EVIL EYE

JEFF SZPIRGLAS

STAR CROSSED PRESS
TORONTO

Library and Archives Canada Cataloguing in Publication

Szpirglas, Jeff
     Evil eye / Jeff Szpirglas.

Also issued in electronic format.
ISBN 978-0-9867914-7-5

     I. Title.

PS8637.Z65E95 2012   jC813'.6   C2012-905705-3 Library and Archives Canada Cataloguing in Publicaton

Summary: After a class trip to the town cemetery Jake's eye begins acting strangely. It's up to Jake to figure out how to stop his new evil eye before it's too late.

Printed and bound in the United States.

FOR LÉO AND RUBY

(AND THEIR BEAUTIFUL NEWBORN EYES)

PROLOGUE

It was the middle of the night, and Jake's eye was on the run.

Well, no. Not *running*. That would be silly. More like floating.

Also, Jake's eye wasn't in his head anymore. Big problem.

The bicycle wobbled as Jake pedalled madly. He pumped his legs up and down. The bike tore down the street, whizzing past stop signs. Ahead, the eye rounded a curve. Jake tried to take it as quickly as the eye, and nearly flew over the handlebars. He hit the brakes and burned a layer of rubber off on the road.

The back tire pushed forward, and Jake had to plant his feet to keep from pitching off the bike.

Up ahead, the eye stopped just under a streetlight.

It hovered in the air like a dragonfly, and turned around to stare at Jake.

Jake shivered.

He could see everything the eye saw. He stood frozen on his bike, watching himself watch himself. The two images bled together. It was hard to separate them. Humans weren't meant to see this way.

Then the eye turned and pressed back into the night. Jake let out a groan, then pushed himself back up on the bike. He pedalled on.

It was almost as if the eye wanted Jake to follow it.

Why else would it keep to the streets? Why else would it stop to let him catch up?

Jake sped on. The road dropped down to a hill, and Jake pedalled as if his life depended on it. The bike raced down the street, picking up as much speed as a car might. The wind tore at his hair and whipped his shirt into ruffles. He squinted his empty eye socket closed and held out his hand. His fingertips were just inches away from the white orb that belonged back in his skull.

He almost had it. Just a few inches more —

The eye swerved out of the way.

It was playing with him.

And Jake knew where it was leading him.

Back to the cemetery.

Jake's head was full of questions, but the biggest one still wasn't answered.

Why?

CHAPTER 1

Jake stepped off the school bus and took a long look around. It was a Monday morning, and he was standing in a cemetery.

It was still early enough in the day and season to see a dusting of frost on the grass. The rising sun was already starting to turn that into a foggy mist that nipped at his ankles. Jake zipped up his coat and shivered. Maybe it was the cold.

Maybe it was something more.

No matter how quiet and peaceful it seemed, a cemetery couldn't hide the fact that it was full of dead people. And somewhere out there, down below the earth, his grandmother rested in her eternal slumber.

Jake's grandmother had died only last year. He could still remember the funeral — remember her coffin going into the ground — remember helping his parents pile the earth on top of it.

And now his teacher, Mr. Glick, had brought the class to this horrible place for some stupid art activity.

Jake shoved his hands into his pockets, doing his very best not to look at his grandmother's tombstone. If he thought too much about her, he might start crying. If he started crying, he'd never hear the end of it from Darryl Richter. This was the worst field trip ever.

"This is the coolest field trip, like, ever!" roared a voice from behind.

Jake turned around. His best friend Jonathan stood there with a grin that seemed to take up his entire face.

Jonathan grabbed Jake and used him like a battering ram to bulldoze their way through the crowd. To Jonathan, the idea of a field trip to the cemetery was, in his own words, "Maybe one of the best ideas in the entire history of human thought."

Jonathan liked scary things. He had inherited a bunch of old horror movie magazines from his older cousin Max. Magazines like *Fangoria* and *Gorezone*, full of pictures of monsters from the bloodiest movies imaginable. His bedroom was plastered with posters of vampires and demons, and crawling with rubber snakes and spiders. He usually brought them to class and shoved them into other students' desks, and then recorded the screams they caused on his smart phone. Freaking people out was Jonathan's calling in life.

He liked to freak his parents out best of all. Three weeks ago Jonathan had dyed his hair jet black, totally goth style. As a consequence, his parents made him cut most of it off. Now he sported an uneven buzz cut that he hid behind a tight-fitting toque. It looked even scarier than the dyed black hair ever did.

Taking Jonathan to a cemetery was about the best thing school could offer him. "Do you know what's under the ground?" he asked Lindsay, who was already bored and standing with her friends underneath a nearby tree.

4

Lindsay pretended not to hear Jonathan. Most people did. Still, she found that ignoring Jonathan only made him ask more weird questions. Seeing that Jonathan was staring her in the face, she gave up. "Dead people?" she tried, hoping her answer would end his line of questioning.

"Not just dead people! Don't get me started, Lindsay. You've got the freshly dead, who are all rotten with bugs and maggots crawling around inside them. Then you've got the ones who are all leathery skin and bone and their internal organs all gone. Then you've —"

"All right already, stop! You're making me sick!"

Jonathan bowed. "It appears my work here is done." He grinned. "Let's continue this at lunchtime, when I shall inform you of the allowable number of insect parts found in everyday groceries …"

A piercing whistle sounded from behind.

Jake, still thinking about his grandmother, jumped.

Most people jumped.

Mr. Glick had a habit of using a whistle to get his students' attention. He never noticed that suddenly blowing on a whistle made everyone jump in shock. "I can tell you're thrilled to be here on a Monday morning," he started. "As you know, we're here to collect etchings!"

Mr. Glick was excited about this field trip, but Mr. Glick was excited about everything. "When you're finished, you can laze around in this park and study for your math test tomorrow! How exciting will that be?"

He was greeted with a deafening silence.

Mr. Glick wrinkled his brow. "Tell you what, the first person who can find my grandfather's tombstone and make an etching of it will get a bonus point on the test tomorrow.

He was a teacher at our school too, you know. In fact, I'm named after him."

"Only one bonus point?" Lindsay asked. "That's nothing."

Mr. Glick pursed his lips and nodded. "You're right. *Two* bonus points!"

To a student like Lindsay, who didn't even need to study for a math test, two extra points was like getting two extra Corn Flakes.

To Jake, this was a different story.

Math was difficult this year. Trying to figure out how to add fractions made his brain hurt. Two extra points might save him from flunking the test. So now, he and Jonathan had a mission.

Mr. Glick started handing out pieces of rubbing paper and sticks of charcoal.

Jake made his way over to Mr. Glick, with Jonathan in tow.

"Have fun." Mr. Glick smiled at the two of them. Then Mr. Glick narrowed his eyes at Jonathan. "You wouldn't be thinking of wandering off, would you?"

"Wander off? *Moi?*"

"If I could hand out grades for wandering off, you would get an A."

"Wow, thanks!"

Mr. Glick rolled his eyes and turned to Jake. "You're Jonathan's partner," he said. "The cemetery is very large, and you'll need to be back before we leave. Make sure the two of you come back in twenty minutes."

Jake nodded. "I will, Mr. Glick."

As Jake and Jonathan moved away, Jake suddenly heard

his words repeated in a shrill, whiny voice: "*I will, Mr. Glick.*"

Jake didn't need anyone to tell him where those words came from. He didn't need to look far, either.

Darryl Richter stood a good head taller than most of his classmates. For whatever reason, he had it in for Jake.

Actually, that's not true. Darryl always had the same reason.

"Because you're such a wimp!" he would laugh.

The problem with Darryl Richter was that most people went along with anything he said. Being big and scary-looking had that kind of effect on people.

And as if to prove it, his two best friends, Malcolm Opal and Horace Hobart, would start laughing, as if everything Darryl Richter said was comedy gold.

Most bullies, in Jake's experience, were pretty dumb. After a lot of pushing and shoving, they usually got caught or in trouble. But Darryl Richter was one of those students who could do no wrong in the teachers' eyes, even with the gum chewing. Darryl Richter was always chewing gum. He'd stick wads of the stuff under desks, in girls' hair, and twice this year on Jake's seat. Mr. Glick had never called Darryl on it, even though the evidence was always right in his mouth. Or stuck elsewhere inside the classroom. That just made things worse.

As far as Jake was concerned, Darryl Richter's number one hobby was making Jake's life miserable.

It had started a few years ago when Jake and Darryl were on the same hockey team. Jake, the meekest defence-man to ever grace the sport, always let the puck fly past him. It wasn't his fault he hadn't learned how to stop properly on skates. Nobody on his hockey team wanted him there. Not even the coach. Jake spent most of his hockey career sitting on the bench.

Things got even worse when Jake's grandmother had to carpool him and Darryl together. She came into the dressing room to lace up Jake's skates. Totally uncool. Then she said the thing that made Jake cringe: "Maybe your friend Darryl can come over for a playdate after the game."

Maybe Jake's grandmother didn't hear the laughter, but Jake did.

The next day at school, all Jake heard were comments about "playdates."

Thus began Darryl Richter's torment of Jake.

Right now, Darryl Richter was turning the etching paper into an airplane and aiming it at Jake's head.

"Come on," Jonathan huffed. "Let's get out of here before he figures out how to actually fold a piece of paper. He might do some origami on us ..."

Darryl clenched his fist. "I heard that."

"Wow, they finally cleaned the wax out of your ears!" Jonathan gawked. "Did they use a jackhammer?"

Jake's mouth dropped. He turned to Jonathan. "Don't ..."

The damage was done. "I'm going to get you," Richter snapped. "Both of you."

"Not in front of Mr. Glick, you won't." Jonathan grinned. Then he waved to Mr. Glick and dashed off between the rows of tombstones.

Jake was left standing in front of Darryl Richter and his cronies.

He smiled and waved at them sheepishly. "That Jonathan ... such a kidder."

"Better get used to this place," Darryl growled, "'cause I'm going to give you a premature burial." He pounded his fist a couple of times.

Jake ran off.

Trying to find Jonathan in an old graveyard was no easy task. Jonathan was already lost amongst the rows of tombstones, probably snapping photographs and coming up with ideas for zombie movies he wanted to make with his video camera.

Jake sprinted past the tombstones, scanning in all directions. The sun was so high in the sky that he had to squint.

Jake finally stopped in his tracks to catch his breath. "Jonathan?!"

"Hey, Jake, check this out!"

Jake whirled around. He couldn't find Jonathan anywhere. "Where are you?"

"Down here!"

Jake stepped beyond the last row of tombstones. The ground dropped away to form a steep hill.

Hill? More like a cliff. Down below, Jonathan was standing by some trees in the distance.

"What are you doing?"

"I found something totally cool."

Jake looked at the hill. He could see where Jonathan's shoes had slipped in the mud. A fierce row of jagged rocks cut through the ground below.

"No way," he said, and abruptly turned away. But he didn't storm off as he had intended. Instead, Jake wrinkled his brow. He returned to the edge of the hill. "How cool is it?" Curiosity was always his downfall.

"See for yourself!"

Jake looked over his shoulder. Most of the class was near the entrance to the cemetery. He checked his watch. It was almost time to head back to the bus. Earlier that year, on their field trip to the museum, Jonathan had gone looking for mummies, and he and Jake had nearly missed the bus. If Jake didn't go down there and grab Jonathan, nobody would. Jake groaned.

"How do I get down?"

"Grab hold of the tree roots. It'll be fun."

Fun? Explaining the mud stains to his mom was never fun. And every time Jake went exploring someplace new, there were always mud stains. Especially when Jonathan was involved.

Holding his hands out for balance, Jake edged down the hill. He bent down low to grab the first tree root he could get a handle on. He pulled on it to make sure it could take his weight, then started to lower himself down.

So far, so good. Jake grinned. Maybe this wasn't going to turn out to be another one of Jonathan's bad ideas after all.

The tree root snapped.

Jake doubled over and tumbled down the hill.

He saw ground. Then sky. Then ground. Then sky. Then ground. Then those jagged rocks. They were coming his way. Fast.

Jake covered up to protect himself. The rocks looked sharp enough to tear through skin, maybe even snap a bone.

Jake closed his eyes, gritted his teeth, then bumped into something heavy.

He looked up.

Jonathan towered over him. He helped Jake get up to his feet. "About time, Jake. We have a bus to get back to, you know."

Jake shook his head. The world was spinning around him. "Please tell me I'm not covered in mud."

Jonathan shrugged. "You chose a bad day to wear a white shirt."

"Great."

"And you've got a big brown smear on the seat of your pants."

"Even better."

"It looks like poo," Jonathan mused. Then he bent down to sniff the smear on Jake's pants. "*Actually...*" he started.

Jake waved him off. "Just show me what you wanted to show me so we can get out of here," he said, moping. He didn't even know how they were going to climb up the hill.

Jonathan pointed ahead.

Jake looked.

For once, Jonathan had found something worth falling down a hill for.

CHAPTER 2

From the top of the hill you couldn't see it properly. But here, at the bottom, Jake could only stare in amazement.

Trees hid another part of the cemetery. It wasn't nearly as big, but far more interesting. The jagged rocks Jake had nearly fallen into were in fact old, shattered tombstones. Several more jutted out of the ground at weird, freakish angles. They looked like a set of morbid dominoes in the middle of falling over.

The tombstones were a lot older than the ones up above. Letters were so worn that it was impossible to make out the names. Or even the language, come to that. Time and the elements had weathered the stones down so much that you couldn't really read anything on them.

"Do you think Mr. Glick's grandfather is buried here?" Jonathan joked, elbowing Jake in the arm.

Jake looked back over his shoulder. "There's no ramp or stairs to get down here. It's totally cut off from the rest of the cemetery. Why would anyone build a cemetery you can't get to?" He felt the kind of chill that wasn't based on the temperature. "Let's go back."

"Are you kidding me? This place is awesome! I could film a slasher movie here. We need to get some pictures for my blog!"

Jonathan dug into his pocket for his smart phone and started taking shots of the tombstones.

"Weren't you supposed to leave that thing at home?"

Jonathan laughed and took a few more pictures. "You know me and rules." He disappeared into the woods, snapping shots of tombstones and trees like they were going out of style.

Jake could see that the trees were different here. They hadn't been planted in a planned manner, like the trees in the cemetery above. It was hard to tell what species they were. These seemed more like the jungle variety, with twisted roots and impossibly angled trunks. It was as if the trees were fighting themselves as they grew.

Up ahead, Jake noted a lone patch of sunlight poking through the branches.

"Jonathan?"

There was no answer. Jake looked at his watch. They were going to be late. This was turning into the museum field trip all over again.

Jake grumbled to himself. His clothes were a mess, and he was going to get in trouble. There was no way his mom would let this one go without some kind of grounding.

Jake strode towards the sunlight. He pushed his way through the foliage, and then stopped in his tracks.

He was standing at the edge of a small, circular clearing in the woods. It was as if the earth itself had been poisoned. Dead weeds and nettles littered the ground. In the centre of the clearing, they formed a large mound.

Jake took a step into the clearing and felt another one of those chills. There was no breeze, and the sun was high in the sky, but something felt wrong. In the new cemetery above, the birds were busy chirping their spring songs. This older cemetery, and this circular clearing in particular, was silent.

The voice in Jake's head was screaming at him to get away, but for some reason, as soon as he had stepped into the circle, Jake had heard another inside voice.

This voice was not his own. It was as if somebody had shoved a second person inside his head.

Closer, the whispery voice urged him.

Jake stepped further into the circle.

Closer, the voice whispered again.

Jake looked over his shoulder. Jonathan was now at the edge of his peripheral vision, snapping more pictures of tombstones. Jake opened his mouth to try to tell Jonathan about this weird mound-thing, but the voice in his head wouldn't let him.

He turned back to the mound.

It looked like someone had gathered a bunch of weeds and nettles and dumped them into a chest-high pile. A pair of narrow, pointed stone blades poked out of either side. They reminded Jake of the pointed tips on top of Batman's cowl. Obviously, Jake had to investigate. Especially with that voice beckoning him to come *closer*.

As he stepped forward, Jake could see that the old weeds and nettles weren't just growing in one big clump. They were covering something.

Jake leaned in. He stuck his hands into the tangle of weeds and pulled them aside. The weeds scratched at the flesh of his fingers, but he had to see inside — had to *feel* inside — the voice wanted him to. Ordered him to.

His fingers brushed against something cold and hard.

Another shiver surged down Jake's spine. He straightened up. He would have turned around and marched off then and there, but that voice —

You've found me.

Found who? Jake couldn't even make out if the voice was male or female. All he could see was …

He was staring at a tombstone.

Again, Jake felt like calling out to Jonathan, but the new voice in his head didn't want him to. Jake wasn't sure what it wanted. The voice was too faint, but it was there, on the edge of his range of hearing. Jake strained to hear the words, so low that he almost thought they had sprung from his own imagination.

Need your help …

Jake shivered again. He didn't want to listen to this voice anymore. It wasn't his. If anything, the voice belonged to whatever was buried under this tombstone.

Still, Jake could not stop himself from pulling away the rest of the weeds. He had to see it. Had to touch it. Maybe if he made an etching …

Jake dug into his pocket for the piece of charcoal and the rubbing paper. He pulled out the paper, unfolded it, and got to work. All he could do with the charcoal was to rub a patch of black on the piece of paper. No etching came through, because there were no letters on the tombstone. Weird. Maybe there was writing elsewhere on the tombstone, but Jake had pulled the weeds away from the centre of the stone. The one place Jake figured you would find writing.

Something behind him blocked out the light, putting

him into shadow.

"I'm almost done, Jonathan."

"Oh, you're done, all right."

Jake straightened up.

It was Darryl Richter. Jake was staring and couldn't bring himself to break eye contact. Darryl had the unblinking face of a reptile. There was no real emotion to be found there, except for a brutish sort of hatred. Darryl held his gaze, chomping on a piece of gum.

Standing behind Richter were Malcolm and Horace, holding Jonathan tightly in their arms.

Jake backed away.

"I don't see Mr. Glick anywhere. Do you?"

Jake shook his head.

"Looks like you made yourself a little etching. Mind if I see?"

Without waiting for an answer, Darryl snatched the etching from Jake and gave it a long look. Then he spit his gum into it and crumpled the paper.

Behind him, Malcolm and Horace laughed as if this was the funniest thing in the world.

Jake gulped. "What do you want?"

Darryl shrugged. "I forgot to give you something."

"Like what?"

"This," he said, throwing the balled-up paper to the ground.

Jake dropped to his knees to pick it up. Another chorus of laughter erupted from behind him.

"He's got mud all over his bum!" Horace yelped.

"Is it mud, or is it, you know, an *accident*?" Malcolm chimed in.

Down on the ground, Jake fumed. He was sick of all the bullying, the name-calling, and the endless, endless wedgies.

Get them, the voice urged him. It was louder now. And angrier.

Jake wrinkled his brow. Was the voice actually telling him what to do?

Stop thinking and get them now. Quickly. They won't expect it ...

Get them? How?

It was hard to hear the voice over the laughter from behind and the sound of Jonathan struggling.

Get them.

Jake stood up. He faced Darryl, and did not turn away.

Fighting back was wrong. Jake knew that. How many times had his parents warned him to find other ways to solve his problems? Something inside him didn't feel like listening. Not this time.

"Looks like you want to punch me." Darryl grinned.

Jake clenched his fist. He'd never been a fighter. Even in hockey he'd been put on defence. Normally he just counted to ten to let the anger fade away, but it was surging inside him now, and the voice in his head kept at him: *Get him. Get him now. He won't be ready for it.*

Jake took a swing.

It was like something else was controlling him. He watched his arm slice through the air. It moved with more power than he'd ever known. And it felt *good*.

He missed Darryl completely. Because he'd never thrown a punch before, Jake didn't count on such a hard follow-through. The momentum made him jerk his leg forward, and his feet got knotted in the tangle of weeds.

He took a step, lost his balance, and fell.

Jake's eyes widened as the sharp edge of one of the tombstone's spiky tips came crashing into view, and —

Whump!

Jake lay writhing on the muddy earth.

"Quick, let's get out of here!" Darryl snapped.

Down on the ground, Jake listened to the three bullies storm off, leaving Jonathan at his feet.

"Jake, you okay?"

Jake clutched at his eye. Already he could feel the surrounding tissues swell. His eye boiled with tears. The pain was so intense that Jake could barely bring himself to breathe.

CHAPTER 3

Things quickly went from bad to worse.

Jonathan helped Jake up the hill, only to find Mr. Glick and the rest of the class busy looking for them.

"There they are!" Lindsay shouted. "All covered in mud."

Mr. Glick and a small crowd of class pets came storming up to greet the two of them. Seeing Jake's hand clamped over his eye, Mr. Glick bent down to get a better look at him. "What happened?"

"Darryl Richter happened, that's what!" Jake blurted.

"He *hit* you? In the eye?" Mr. Glick looked around for any sign of Darryl.

Darryl and his friends had been there. They were all witnesses. It was Jake who threw the punch, even if that stupid voice told him to. Voices couldn't get in trouble. While Darryl had started it, Jake would be in as much trouble. He shook his head.

"So what really happened?" Mr. Glick asked.

"I tripped," Jake explained, sniffling back tears.

"Onto your face?"

"No!" Jake snapped, clamping his hand to his eye. "I tripped and fell, and my eye hit one of the tombstones. The pointy end."

Mr. Glick leaned in close, so only Jake might hear him. "But Jake, none of these tombstones have any pointy ends."

Jake pulled his hand away and tried to stare at Mr. Glick as best as he could. His eye was watering so badly that he couldn't really focus on Mr. Glick, or the growing crowd around him.

"You must have fallen on something *else*," Mr. Glick suggested.

Jake shrugged. What did it matter? Why was Mr. Glick making such a big deal out of it?

"Let's get you back to school," Mr. Glick said reassuringly.

The rest of the class piled onto the bus while Mr. Glick quickly phoned the school.

Jake's mom was already waiting to take him to the hospital when the bus pulled in to the front drive of the school. As usual, she gave him a big hug and told him everything was going to be all right.

Then she started asking questions, like how the mud stains got on his pants. Jake wasn't really one for making good excuses.

He told the truth instead.

"What possessed you to go down a steep hill into the mud?" his mother asked. "You could have really hurt yourself."

"I *am* really hurt," he told her.

"So what happened to your eye, then?"

He wanted to tell her about Darryl Richter, but Jake had

been the one to throw the punch. What had Richter done, other than take his etching and spit in it?

Once they got to the hospital, Jake sat in the waiting room. Other people were milling about, some doubled over in pain, most looking just plain bored. Jake's eye was watering too much for him to read any of the magazines on the table, and he couldn't focus on the tiny television set hanging from the wall.

It was at least an hour before Jake was seen by the doctor, who immediately sat him down on an observation table. Separating Jake from the table was a paper sheet to keep the table free from germs. The sheet was big enough to etch at least three tombstones, but Jake couldn't think about etching now.

"Can you open your eye for me?"

The doctor's voice was calm and soothing, but Jake's eye was burning. It felt like someone had pressed it against the red-hot coil of a stove. He shook his head.

"Jake," the doctor started again, "I need to see your eye in order to know what's wrong with it."

"It hurts, that's what's wrong with it!" Jake sniffled back tears. He'd shed some because he was scared, because his eye felt like a volcano, but mostly because Darryl Richter was pure evil.

The doctor shone a light at Jake's face, and he clenched his eyelids shut. The doctor got desperate: "If you open your eye for me, maybe you'll get a lollipop."

Jake opened his other eye to see whether or not the doctor was joking. How old did this guy think Jake was?

Nothing happened for a while after that. At some point, Jake opened both eyes. Big mistake. The doctor forced the bad eye open with his thumb and index finger and shone a light into it. Jake clenched his teeth. His eye felt like it was going to explode out of its socket. If it did, Jake hoped it would spew all over the doctor.

"I thought so," the doctor told Jake's mom, who had been sitting nearby. "He's scratched his cornea."

Scratched? Cornea? That sounded bad. "Is it serious?" Jake demanded.

The doctor patted Jake on the back. "You'll be fine," he started, "but you'll have to wear a patch."

"That's cool," Jake said, and tried to smile.

"See?" the doctor grinned. "No problem."

Jake sat there and tried to imagine how cool he was going to look with the eye patch. He figured it would be one of those black patches pirates and scary motorcycle dudes wore.

"Hang on one sec," the doctor chirped, and turned around.

Jake tried to look over his shoulder to see the patch. Did they keep them in drawers around here or something?

"Here we are!" the doctor exclaimed, and turned around with his hands full of gauze and surgical tape.

"What's that?"

"Your patch."

"But it's just bandages, and —"

Before Jake could finish talking, the doctor grabbed hold of his head, jammed the gauze over his bad eye, and fastened it on with what felt like twenty pieces of white surgical tape.

When it was done, the doctor handed Jake a mirror. "What do you think?"

"I look like an idiot."

The doctor shrugged. "Could be worse," he mused.

"How's that?"

22

"You could have scratched *both* eyes."

What Jake also hadn't expected was losing his depth perception.

"You need both of your eyes to make things look three-dimensional," the doctor told him. "With only one eye, the world might appear more flat than usual."

The doctor seemed to be able to read Jake's mind. "Don't worry, Jake." He smiled reassuringly. "I'm sure you'll be right as rain in no time."

So he was going to have to wear this silly patch for a day or two. He wasn't supposed to read or write with the patch on because it might strain his good eye.

Hang on a second!

If he couldn't read or write, then how the heck was he going to write the upcoming math test?

Maybe this whole eye patch thing wasn't so bad after all.

The next day, Jonathan caught up with Jake on the way to school.

"Nice patch, Jake! That looks awesome."

"Really?"

Jonathan shook his head. "No, not really. I'm just trying to be positive. But at least you got out of having to write the test. For now, at least."

"You're never in a good mood on math test days," Jake observed. He narrowed his good eye at Jonathan. "Why the change?"

Jonathan shrugged.

"Tell me," Jake urged.

"Tell you *what?*"

"How are you going to try to cheat on the test this time?"

"You think I'd try to chea—"

"Yes, I do."

"Okay, you got me there." Jonathan dug into his pocket and pulled out his phone. He turned it on and revealed a series of pictures he'd taken right out of the math textbook.

"Good idea, isn't it? The phone's a lot smaller than the textbook. I figure when Glick's not looking, I'll just zoom in on one of these pictures and figure out how to solve a question. I even organized the pictures by subject." Jonathan seemed really proud of himself.

"You put a lot of thought into this," Jake mused.

"*Hours*," Jonathan admitted. He got a faraway look in his eyes. "I guess I could have spent the time studying, but that wouldn't be nearly as fun."

Jake rolled his eyes. "One of these days, you're going to get burned."

"Hey, if you never play with matches, how can you make fire?"

Jake shook his head. "I don't think that's how the saying goes."

Jonathan waved Jake off. "If I spent my time trying to remember old sayings, I'd never learn the new ones. Come on."

As Jake and Jonathan reached the schoolyard, all sorts of students started coming up to them: kids in their class, kids in other classes. Everybody had something to say, mostly because Jake was the kind of person people felt like they could say anything to.

"What happened to your eye?"

"You look like the Mummy."

"Did you put the gauze factory out of business?"

"Too bad you missed the other eye."

This last line came from Darryl Richter, who stood behind a crowd with his usual gang of cretins, Horace and Malcolm.

Jake looked past the crowd of onlookers and stared Darryl down. He clenched a fist and his teeth. Anger surged. Under the gauze, his scratched eye twitched.

"Oh, look. He's staring at you!" Malcolm chortled. "Maybe he wants to try to punch you again."

"Yeah, you'd better not punch him," Horace reminded Jake. "The school's got rules about that kind of stuff."

Jake kept his good eye locked on Richter. Normally, Jake would've turned his eyes to the ground, but not now. He was too flooded with rage.

Jake took a few deep breaths. It was a new feeling, this Not Looking Away. He wished he could tear off the gauze bandage and stare Darryl down with both eyes.

As it turned out, he didn't need to.

It was Darryl Richter who broke the gaze, casting his eyes to the pavement below.

"Come on," he hissed. "Let's get out of here before Freak-Eye starts to cry or something …"

Jonathan turned to Jake. "Whoa. Did you see him walk away like that? What did you just *do*?"

Jake shrugged.

The classroom walls were covered with tombstone etchings that Mr. Glick had posted proudly. They flapped in the breeze Jake and his classmates made walking to their desks.

"This place is creepy," Lindsay muttered.

"So is your hair," Jonathan said from behind. Lindsay

rolled her eyes and muttered something about "boys," then got to her seat. The students were seated in rows, and Jonathan's desk was right behind Lindsay's. It was kind of weird the way he always ended up a few seats away from her, no matter how much Mr. Glick seemed to change the seating plan.

After taking attendance and standing for the national anthem, Mr. Glick had everyone separate their desks for the math test.

Jake's seat was far from Jonathan and Lindsay's, and only a few away from Darryl Richter's. For some reason, it felt like Jake's desk was always near Darryl's, no matter how many times Mr. Glick rearranged the seating plan.

Mr. Glick paced about the classroom and handed out the math test. He stopped at Jake's desk. "And what are we going to do with you?"

Jake shrugged. "I scratched my eye." He handed Mr. Glick the doctor's note he'd been given.

Mr. Glick scanned the note. "Hmmm," he muttered.

"The doctor said it might be tricky for me to read too much," Jake added. It was true. The doctor had kept assuring Jake that he'd be "right as rain," and that he could decide whether or not he wanted to take a day off school. Jake wanted to stay home, but his parents didn't want him missing anything important.

Instead, he had to come here and watch everyone else write the math test.

Jake looked on as the rest of the class got started. A nervy silence descended upon the room, broken only by the scratching of pencils against paper and the shuffling of feet under desks. There was the odd rattle of a pencil in a desk, or the squeak of an eraser rubbing out a mistake. All the while, Mr. Glick surveyed the room like a sentinel, standing in place, his gaze circling like the beacon on a lighthouse.

Jake turned his attention to Jonathan.

Jonathan's eyes were on Mr. Glick. He watched the way Mr. Glick surveyed the students, trying to pick out a pattern to the teacher's wandering gaze. In order to cheat, Jonathan needed to figure out the right time to break out his smart phone without getting caught.

Jake watched as Jonathan slowly reached into his desk and pulled out the phone. Jonathan's eyes barely left Mr. Glick, who now had his attention on Darryl Richter. Jonathan's fingers switched the phone on, causing a dim blue glow to come from his desk as it powered up.

There was a knock at the door. Some second-grader was standing there. "Miss Dziak wants to borrow your stapler!" she exclaimed as if having rehearsed it. Mr. Glick turned his attention to the kid and, consequently, in Jonathan's direction. Jonathan reacted nervously, arms locking into place. A huge burst of light from the camera's flash blazed from the desk, causing several more heads to turn in Jonathan's direction.

Mr. Glick cleared his throat.

Darryl looked away innocently.

Mr. Glick walked over to Jonathan and held out his hand. "The camera, please."

Jonathan looked perplexed. "*Camera?* What camera?"

Just as Mr. Glick began to turn an angry shade of crimson, Jonathan let out a sigh and handed his teacher the phone. He looked down at the test before him and cradled his head in his hands. He managed a sideways glance to Jake.

Several rows away, Jake shrugged, as if to say, "I told you so."

He then shifted his focus. He kept his good eye trained on Mr. Glick, who moved to the classroom window. Mr. Glick turned the crank that opened the window. A cool breeze filtered into the room, rustling papers.

Lindsay raised her hand. "Can you close the window, Mr. Glick? It's really cold."

"Cool air will make you think," Mr. Glick returned, his gaze lingering on Jake.

Jake fidgeted uncomfortably in his seat, and turned his attention to Darryl Richter writing the math test.

Darryl was also shifting in his seat. He kept shifting his gaze from the test to the clock, but the clock didn't have the answers. It could only tick at him. Darryl chewed on the end of his pencil. He ran his fingers through his hair. He put his hand up to ask a question. When Mr. Glick shook his head, Darryl lowered his hand. He huffed and puffed. Finally, Darryl looked over the shoulder of the girl ahead of him for the answers, but Mr. Glick was watching.

"Why don't you finish up in the study carrel?" he asked Darryl, pointing to the desk at the back of the room.

Darryl turned around to see Jake smiling. "What are you looking at, Long Jake Silver?!" he blurted. The whole class burst out laughing.

Jake wasn't smiling anymore.

And his eye started to sting again.

That night, Jake had one of those dreams where you lift away from your body and go floating about.

He'd never actually had one of those dreams before, but

28

he'd heard of them. Most of his dreams usually involved getting pummelled in hockey, or showing up to school in his underpants. Both of these things had actually happened to him.

This dream was different. He rose away from his own body until he was staring down at himself. It was weird to see his sleeping form. His body was turned to the side so his face was hidden. Jake hovered there for a moment, watching the steady rise and fall of his own chest.

Jake turned and floated through his room. The details of the dream world were exactly the same as in the real world, from the Lego building on his desk to the video game posters on the wall.

The clarity of the details wasn't the only strange thing about the dream. Usually his dreams came in weird flashes, but this one flowed as if it were actually happening. But it couldn't be happening, not the way Jake drifted down to the carpet level and pushed his way through the crack under the door.

Jake wasn't sure how he could fit through the crack. Maybe in this dream he was as thin as the rubbing paper he'd etched that tombstone with.

Jake floated down the staircase to the front door. Near the bottom was a swinging flap for the mail delivery. Jake pushed himself through, and with a metallic clink it fell behind him and he was outside.

Night cloaked the street in a blanket of pure dark, like chimney soot. It was only early spring, and the nights were still cool. Normally he'd be shivering, but he couldn't feel the cold against his body.

Jake breezed down the street. All he had to do was visualize rising into the air and he did so. He could float as high as he wanted, or descend as low to the ground as he liked. It was kind of fun. Who wouldn't want the power to fly?

A pair of headlights emerged at the end of the street. Jake immediately swerved and took shelter behind some nearby bushes until the car drove past. When the red tail lights disappeared behind him, Jake came out from the bushes and continued to float on. Something was telling him to be cautious.

So, where to next?

There was nobody on the street, except for a few outdoor cats that eyed him curiously.

Most house lights were off, but Jake noticed one in an upstairs room just across the street. Jake floated over to the window to take a look inside.

An old woman sat up in her bed, reading a book. It wasn't the most interesting thing to spy on in a dream, but it was better than nothing. He moved in more closely.

There seemed to be rules to this dream. Up until now, he'd been squeezing through cracks under doors, or through the mail slot, as if he were made up of actual substance. But that couldn't be right. Why couldn't he pass through closed windows or doors? It was worth a shot.

Jake moved back, to give himself a burst of speed, and then soared straight for the window.

Smack!

Jake wanted to scream or cry out, but no sound came. All he could feel was a stabbing pain in his eye. He'd not been able to clear the window, but he'd hit it with enough force to make the old woman take notice. She put her book down, and turned to look at him.

The old woman squinted at first. Why was she squinting? Couldn't she see him?

Jake hung by the window, wondering what she might do next.

The old woman got out of bed and walked to the window.

When she and Jake were eye to eye the old woman let out a scream. Her windows must have been really thick, because Jake couldn't hear one tiny bit of it.

Jake hovered off, losing himself in the thick of the night.

As he made his way back onto the main street, Jake wondered why he'd spent so much time outside the old woman's window. Why had it taken her so long to see him? Had he developed the power to shrink in this dream, too?

A thought occurred to Jake.

He had the power to float. He could squeeze into small spaces. And tomorrow, he was going to have to write that math test.

Jake knew exactly where he wanted to go next.

It didn't take him long to reach the school. He circled it like a vulture. The doors were locked. The windows were shut —

No. Not all of them. One of the windows was open. Just a sliver. Just enough to let some fresh air in, and enough space for Jake to squeeze through, too.

He floated his way through the halls, finally stopping outside room 4B. As with his own bedroom door, Jake floated down to the gap between the bottom of the door and the floor and squeezed inside.

Squeezed?

Yes, Jake could feel the pressure of the door against him. So he did have solid form in this crazy dream.

Now he was in his own classroom, floating past the rows of desks to the heavy table that Mr. Glick sat behind. Sitting atop the desk was a bundle of stapled papers. It was the math test, fully marked.

Jake couldn't believe it.

Because this was a dream, and not real life, Jake took note of all the questions on that test, and the right answers.

This was cheating, wasn't it? Jake had never even thought of cheating before in his life.

Yet there was something pushing Jake to look at the tests and the answers. Something like a voice. Like a whisper in his head.

A voice like the one he'd heard in the dead circle by that tombstone.

Jake couldn't make out what it was trying to tell him.

It didn't really matter, did it? This wasn't cheating. It was just a dream.

CHAPTER 4

"Wake up, sleepyhead. Time to get ready for school."

Jake opened his eyes, but only one of them could blink his mother into focus.

The other was still smothered under the gauze and surgical tape of his eye patch. "Can I take this thing off yet?" he asked.

"It looks like you've already started."

"What do you mean?"

Jake reached up and felt around his face. The surgical tape holding the patch had torn off on one side. Jake wondered if he'd sweated in his dream so much that the tape had loosened. But why did it loosen only in one corner?

"You must have done that in your sleep."

Jake, still not quite awake, simply shrugged. "Can I take the rest of this thing off?"

"Sure. Your eye should be healed by now."

Jake got out of bed and thumped over to the bathroom. He wasn't a big fan of pulling off bandages. He soaked the skin covered with the bandage in warm water to loosen the adhesive. Then, with a few gentle tugs, he pulled the bandage off smoothly and cleanly, without ripping out any hairs or pulling too tightly on the skin.

Jake blinked a bit. He'd almost grown used to manoeuvring in the world that had its dimensions flattened. With two eyes working again, all of the details popped out in their proper three dimensions. After being closed for so long, everything now looked unnaturally bright through his healed eye.

A fly buzzed against the windowpane. It crawled through a hole in the screen window and then flew up to the ceiling. Jake tracked the fly as it flew from one corner of the bathroom to another. He was able to scan about the room more easily than he had before getting his cornea scratched. The eye felt a little different now, but *good*.

"How are you feeling?" Jake's mother asked when he came downstairs to the kitchen. She was already downing a cup of steaming coffee and some burnt toast. Jake fished through the cabinet for a box of cereal and dumped a helping into a bowl.

"Good as new."

Jake got on with the morning routine. He changed out of his pajamas and into his clothes. He went upstairs and brushed his teeth. Then he got his things together and made his way to school.

Sometimes Jake would take his bike to school; mostly he just walked. For one thing, Jake's bike was a dorky-looking mustard yellow one that Darryl Richter called the "Big Banana."

Besides, Jake enjoyed the walk. It allowed him to gather his thoughts, or run through episodes of cool TV shows, or even just let his mind wander. Jake had always been a daydreamer.

He found Jonathan in his usual spot on the far side of the school opposite the playground. It was where the two boys hung out. Nobody came back here — not students, not even teachers on duty. There was only one door back here, and that was the entrance for the caretaker, Mr. Roberts. He only popped his head out here if he wanted to have a cigarette, but he never did that during school hours.

It was a good spot if you wanted to keep away from bullies, stare at the clouds, or just poke around at an anthill. Jonathan's attention was drawn to the anthill. His focus shifted as he heard Jake approach, and he smiled. "Hey, two-eyes. Nice to see you with stereoscopic vision again."

Jonathan was always saying stuff like that. He had a knack for knowing all sorts of weird trivia.

"Stereo-what?"

"Stereoscopic. Three dimensions. Like in 3D movies. You need both eyes for that."

"Yeah, I know," Jake said. He'd already gotten used to trying to make his way through the world with one eye.

Jake was preoccupied with the world around him. He seemed to be able to focus better on the insects hopping from grass-blade to grass-blade. He could track the movements of all the flying bugs, and even keep count of the ants on the anthill. It wasn't that things *looked* any different. Jake's eye just followed things more quickly. The tiniest movement caught his attention, at least in the one eye.

Jake's gaze fell on Jonathan, who was busy playing with his phone.

"I thought you were supposed to keep that at home."

Jonathan shrugged. "You have no idea how long I've

been working on beating the high score in Minesweeper."

"Mr. Glick will take it away from you."

"Not if I do a better job of hiding it."

"You didn't do such a great job yesterday," Jake said.

"I accidentally took a picture. I won't make the same mistake today," Jonathan returned. "It wasn't even a good picture. Except for the one cool thing I found. See?"

Jake squinted at the fuzzy-looking picture. He found that his newly healed eye brought it into focus quickly. It was of the inside of Jonathan's desk. The photo revealed some dry wads of chewing gum that past students had stuck there. But it was the other detail that stood out — the letters SCRUMB were carved into the wood of the desk.

"'scrumb'? What's that supposed to mean?"

"Who knows? More importantly, why would someone bother carving it into the inside of a desk?"

"Somebody who doesn't want it being seen?" Jake tried.

"I totally get hiding swearing, but 'scrumb'? It doesn't make sense," Jonathan said.

Soon the bell rang. Jake and Jonathan lined up with the rest of the junior students and filed noisily into the classroom.

Once he'd taken his jacket off, Mr. Glick got down to business. One of the first things he did was plop a copy of the math test down on Jake's desk.

Jake looked up to find Mr. Glick grinning at him. "Nice to see you with both eyes again, Jake."

As Mr. Glick moved away, Jake looked down at the test.

No.

It couldn't be.

Jake stared at the top sheet of paper, wondering if he was

still dreaming things.

It was same test he'd seen last night, in his dream.

Jake looked over his shoulder to find Mr. Glick moving back to his desk. Now it really was cheating. He knew all the questions. He'd memorized all the answers. It was impossible, but it had happened. He raised his hand to say something.

His eye started twitching.

It was just a spasm of the muscles around his eye, but it was enough to stop Jake from raising his hand all the way up. He rubbed his eye and blinked it back under control. He went to raise his hand again, but the eye twitched a second time.

Jake blinked his eye open and closed. He looked away from Mr. Glick and back down at the test.

Jake got out of his seat and went to sharpen his pencil. He ground the pencil down to a sharp tip, then made his way to his desk.

He became aware of the voice from the cemetery again. It wasn't making actual words. Instead, Jake realized that the inside voice was thinking his thoughts for him, moving them away from being honest about the test.

Jake wasn't sure why the voice wanted him to cheat, but if that would make it go away, so be it.

He sat down and gave a surprised spasm. Something was on his chair. Something soft, mushy, and …

Jake sat up and felt underneath his bottom.

A wad of chewed gum was stuck to his pants and the seat. The skin around Jake's neck went red-hot and prickled. A surge of pins and needles ran through his body. He clenched his teeth and let out a long breath.

Jake scanned the room, although he knew exactly who had put it there without having to confirm it.

Most of the other students were busy doing their bell work or silent reading. Most, but not all. Darryl Richter was staring at him. *Smiling* at him. And making chewing motions with his mouth.

Then Darryl turned to Horace and Malcolm. The three of them tried their very best not to burst out laughing. A few muffled snorts came through, but not enough to catch Mr. Glick's attention. He was busy moving about the classroom, doing his routine homework check. He'd completely failed to see what had just happened. As usual.

For a moment Jake thought about standing up, marching over to Darryl, and scratching him with the sharp end of the pencil.

No. Not scratching.

Stabbing.

Jake didn't want to picture it, but he couldn't help himself. In his mind, he clutched the pencil and brought it down on Darryl Richter in a stabbing motion. Darryl let out a piercing shriek and fell to the floor, limbs twitching wildly. Jake stood over him, watching him squirm in pain. Watching his eyes bulge out of his head. Watching him take his last breath —

Jake blinked the images out of his head. They were wrong. They were bad. Jake often had revenge fantasies against Darryl and his thugs, but none like this. None so graphic. None in which Darryl was lying down on the floor in critical condition.

Still, Jake felt the gum under his bum. He didn't want to make a big scene out of this. Not in front of everyone else. He reached into his desk for a scrap of paper, then sat up, leaning forward. He could feel the gum pull away from the chair, and imagined it stretching out in globby pink strings from his pants.

Jake reached behind him and tried to wipe away the gum as best he could. Once upon a time he used to love the smell of gum, but now the thick, sweet scent of it made him want to retch.

Later, the voice in his head assured him.

Jake wasn't sure what the voice was getting at. He diverted his attention away from it and tried to remember what he'd seen from the test in his dream.

Normally, he wouldn't be able to remember a dream so vividly. Details like the pages of a math test would have been lost on him, especially after a night's sleep. But as Jake closed his eyes, he formed a mental picture in his head. He could literally see the math test answers.

Jake opened his eyes, looked down at the test, and began to write.

Jake turned and smiled at Darryl Richter. *Later*, the voice had told him.

Jake guessed he would find out what the voice was getting at soon enough.

Jake stopped on his way out of the classroom. His eye twitched to attention at the box of solar-powered calculators that Mr. Glick left out on his desk.

There was nothing noteworthy about them. They were just calculators, but his eye was twitching, and —

Take it.

Jake shook his head. It wasn't his property to take.

You can use it.

Use it for what? What had gotten into his inside voice lately?

Jake shrugged and turned away. He made it about three steps when he found himself stopping, backing up, and looking over his shoulder.

Mr. Glick was busy helping out another student. He wasn't watching. Jake looked over his other shoulder. Nobody was watching.

Nobody could see him when he reached his hand to the box of calculators and pocketed one.

Jake left the class feeling guilty. He'd stolen. It was the first time he'd ever pulled a stunt like that, and it made his insides feel raw.

But then … he could return it, couldn't he? Just bring the calculator back the next morning. Mr. Glick left the case out. It was unlikely he counted them all every day. Nobody would notice if Jake returned the calculator.

Only …

Good work, the voice told him. *But you're going to need even more than that.*

Jake wrinkled his brow. What else would he need?

As he left the room Jake realized that, no, he wasn't going to return the calculator. He was going to steal it, plain and simple.

Something was happening to him. Something he couldn't control or understand.

Jake clenched his fists and shivered.

His eye twitched.

The voice in his head didn't bother him at all during

dinner, or even when he studied for his math test afterwards. It didn't say anything when Jake studied the calculator he'd stolen from Mr. Glick, although Jake knew that it was the voice that had compelled him to do it. But why steal a calculator?

After dinner, Jake excused himself and went outside. He took the key to get into the garage, which stood at the back of the yard beside the shed.

The garage smelled like an auto shop full of oil, old paint, and grime. Jake flipped a switch and a few bulbs flickered to life. The main space of the garage was more or less vacant, save for a lawnmower and a few bicycles that had been taken down from the rafters. To the far side sat a long workbench, a pair of dirty sinks, and a window looking out to the backyard.

Jake reached into his pocket and produced the calculator. He put it on the workbench and fished out a flathead screwdriver from the table. Then he pried open the calculator and regarded its guts.

He'd always been curious to look inside a calculator, but he'd never had the urge to steal one and then crack it open. This was more than curiosity. It was that voice again, urging him on.

Jake's hands began to move as if they knew what they were doing. He found himself grabbing other screwdrivers from the workbench, and a pair of scissors to snip away the circuit board from the plastic casing.

This is a start, the voice inside his head said.

A sudden chill ran down Jake's spine.

"A start for *what*?" he asked aloud, although he wasn't sure he needed to. If the voice was in his mind, maybe it

41

could just read his thoughts.

The voice didn't answer. It didn't speak to him for the rest of the evening. Not when Jake was doing his homework or watching television. Not even when he went to bed and tumbled off into sleep.

The voice even stayed out of his dreams.

Speaking of dreams, this was the second out-of-body dream Jake had had in just as many days.

There he was, floating above his own body. He looked so peaceful sleeping down there in his bed. *But there were things to do.*

Things to do?

Indeed.

Jake didn't need any voice to tell him what to do. This was his dream, and he could do what he liked with it.

It was time to make a visit to Darryl Richter.

CHAPTER 5

Jake still knew where Darryl lived; it was only a few years back that he and Darryl had carpooled to hockey games together. Heck, as far back as the first grade you might have even called the two of them friends.

But Grade 1 was a long time ago.

Now Jake floated outside of Darryl Richter's window. Through the glass pane and the half-drawn blinds, Jake could make out Darryl's sleeping form. He looked so innocent sleeping in his bed. Like he couldn't even harm a fly. (Come to think of it, giving a fly a wedgie is a pretty difficult task.)

For a moment, Jake had second thoughts. This wasn't the right thing to do, and he knew it. Already he'd used this weird new power to cheat on the math test, but to break into Darryl's house wasn't like him. Because that's what this was, breaking in.

Still, something was fuelling Jake that he couldn't quite understand.

Get inside. He won't suspect a thing. Get him and hurt *him.*

Yes, Jake thought to himself. For once, it would be Darryl who would be begging him for mercy. Darryl would be the one grovelling. Darryl could eat his own words. He could eat dirt for all Jake cared. Maybe he would.

Jake circled around the house. It wasn't just Darryl's bedroom window that was closed. All the windows on the upper floor were shut. So were those on the lower level. There had to be another way inside.

Then Jake remembered how he'd left his own house in last night's dream. He'd pushed himself through the mail slot in the door. Quickly, Jake floated over to the front door and spied a similar mail slot. He approached it quietly and carefully. All he had to do was reach over, flip it open, and shove himself inside. He'd be the ultimate piece of junk mail!

That's when Jake noticed a problem.

Despite being within arm's reach of the mail slot, he couldn't move his arm to pull it open.

He tried again. He could feel his arm stretching forward. He could gauge where the mail slot was from his perspective outside the door. But the hand did not meet the mail slot.

Jake realized something else. Looking around the front door for another entrance, it dawned upon him that he'd not seen himself yet. This normally wasn't a problem — unless looking into a mirror, you never get a good look at yourself. But in this dreamy floating state, Jake had not seen one tiny bit of himself. He looked down at the ground for his legs, but they weren't there. He reached his arms out and waved them around in front of his eyes. They too could not be seen.

It didn't make sense. Jake could feel every movement of his body. Yet it would not register in his field of vision.

A dream, Jake told himself. *It's just a dream, and these are the weird rules that go along with it.*

Jake floated away from the door. He was just about to

give up his attempt to get back at Darryl Richter when he caught sight of the chimney poking from the Richters' roof.

If he was small enough to squeeze through the crack under a door, or through a mail slot, then what about the chimney?

Jake flew over to inspect it. A wire mesh covered the chimney cap. He stared down into the shaft below. This was the sort of impossible thing that happened only in dreams, but what the heck. He moved in close and pushed himself through one of the metal squares that formed the mesh.

Cold metal pressed against him.

Instinctively, Jake reached out with his arms to help squeeze inside.

What he felt was something soft.

It wasn't metal.

It was soft and familiar. Certainly not the metal grille he was now squeezing himself through.

Just a little bit more ...

And he was inside the chimney.

Jake could still feel something soft around him, even as he sunk into the depths of the chimney. He had never been down a mineshaft, but figured this couldn't be too far off. Choking black soot caked the narrow walls. Above, the pinprick of light from the moon filtered through the mesh on the chimney cap. But even that light faded the deeper he went.

Soon he could see nothing at all.

In the blackness of the chimney, Jake still felt something soft. It was covering his entire body. Something soft and warm and ...

Jake opened his eyes.

The soft feeling around his body was his own bed and blankets. He breathed in and out for a moment, pushed off the blankets bundling him, and then sat up. He was sweating. His pajamas stuck to his skin. The dream had felt so real, and yet here he was.

Jake glanced at the bedside table. The digital alarm clock read 2:05 a.m. It was the middle of the night, and Jake was thirsty.

He rolled out of bed, his feet padding against the floor. Jake felt dizzy, a bit disoriented. At first, he couldn't quite place it, but soon recognized the sensation. He was lacking depth perception — just like when he'd worn the patch.

Jake blinked. He wasn't wearing a patch anymore, but the room looked as if it had been flattened into two dimensions. He grasped at the doorknob and twisted it open, then made his way down the hallway. He held his hands out to the walls to keep steady and shuffled to the bathroom.

Once inside, Jake closed the door, then filled a cup with water from the tap and gulped it back. The nightlight was bright enough to let Jake look into the mirror.

Urgh. His hair was a mess, his eye was missing —

"Gak!"

Jake dropped the cup. It clattered to the floor, spilling the water.

He shut his eye — *eyes*! He shut his *eyes*.

(And now he could see something in his mind's eye: a shaft of light. It was coming through the bottom of the chimney. Someone had left it open.)

Stop thinking about Darryl's house and open your eyes!

Jake opened them. Messy hair, missing eye. Perfect. Perfect. Per—

46

Why was this so perfect?

Jake answered that one himself: "It's still a dream. Or maybe a nightmare." Now he was smiling about it, because he was going to go back to bed and pull the covers over himself and sleep until morning and then everything would be fine and he'd get up and brush his teeth and two eyes would be staring back at him from the bathroom mirror this time and —

He stared at his reflection. His eye socket was as empty as a doughnut hole. With only the nightlight on, it was too dim to see into the dark pit of the socket. Jake wondered what would happen if he turned the bathroom light on. Would he be able to see into his brain? He resisted the temptation to stick his finger into the gaping hole in his head.

The world around him wanted to spin. This was too much. Jake clutched the cold porcelain of the sink.

Meanwhile, the picture in his mind (the one in Darryl Richter's house) was changing. He'd pushed himself through the chimney and into the fireplace. Thankfully, there was no fire going. He was free to float about the house. It was well past two in the morning and everyone was fast asleep.

Jake could see this in his, what did you call it, his mind's eye?

Only, it wasn't his mind's eye. It was his actual *other* eye. It wasn't in his head. It was in Darryl Richter's house!

Jake concentrated. He could see what the eye was seeing, because although it was floating around in somebody else's house, it was still his eye. He looked through the runaway eye as it floated past the family room, up the stairs—

Jake closed the eye still in his head, and the bathroom mirror was replaced with darkness.

47

But not complete darkness.

Jake could still see out of the floating eye.

It was almost at Darryl Richter's bedroom. Darryl's room was easy to spot. There was a giant sign posted on the door that read: "KEEP OUT."

Even if Darryl had locked the door, he couldn't keep the eye out.

Jake watched as his eye moved down to ground level, found the gap between the door and floor, and then squeezed itself through.

A thought entered Jake's mind. Who was controlling the eye? Was it him? He'd wanted to get revenge on Darryl Richter for, well, just about everything. But as he stood in the bathroom with his eyelids squeezed shut, Jake tried to will his eye back under the door, out of the room.

"Come back to daddy," he whispered.

Yet the eye pressed on.

It floated over to the bed, so that the single orb was staring down over Darryl Richter's sleeping face.

Jake concentrated.

Move away, he told himself. *Move away from Darryl Richter before you get yourself into any further trouble.*

The eye floated on.

Jake breathed a sigh of relief. So he could control this runaway eye after all. Now he just needed to get it out of Darryl's house, get it back here, then figure out what to do next, and —

Back in the bathroom, Jake opened his other eye. He regarded himself in the mirror and leaned in close. He stared in amazement at the hole in the socket where his wandering eye should have been. He could see the muscle and viscera beyond. It was disgusting. Think of something else, he told himself, and then his mind was back in Darryl's room.

Then he saw it. The eye was hovering near a shelf overlooking Darryl's bed. It was a bookcase. The books were held in place by two heavy bookends in the shape of dragons.

The bookends hadn't been placed properly.

Jake shut the eye still in his head to see the picture more clearly.

The books were angled against one bookend. He could see that the bookend was half on the shelf, half off the shelf. All one had to do was push some of the standing books over. Just a little nudge would do it. The books would fall like dominoes. The bookend would fall off the shelf.

Darryl's head was under the shelf.

Jake's face drained of colour.

Don't even think it! But he was. That was just it. Jake *was* thinking it. *Push it over. Just give it a little nudge.*

It was only an eye, but there had to be a brain it worked for.

Whose brain? Was it Jake's? Jake had never found it in himself to hurt anybody. Not even Darryl Richter, and he had good reason to.

Was there something lurking in the back of his mind? Something angry and furious from all the bullying? Was there some part of his brain that wanted a little revenge?

Maybe more than a little.

He could control that part of his mind. He'd controlled it his whole life. Mind your manners, work hard at your studies, be polite to strangers, and control your temper ...

He focused his mind to one pinprick of thought. *Get out of Darryl's room*, he told himself, over and over again. *You can do it. Move away from the shelf, slip back under the door, out the mail slot.*

But his other eye just kept staring at the shelf. Then the eye looked from Darryl sleeping in the bed back to the bookend.

Get out of there, he willed his eye.

For a moment, it seemed like his eye was obeying him. It hovered away from the shelf.

The eye stopped. It turned abruptly so it was facing the first bookend.

Then it sped forward, gaining momentum. Jake could only watch helplessly as the eye slammed into the bookend.

Pain surged through the nerves around his eye!

Jake clenched his teeth and tried to suppress the scream he desperately wanted to let out. He staggered back, his head pounding. Although the eye was not in his head, his nerves were. He could feel what it felt.

Back in Darryl's room, the bookend knocked into the first book. The first book fell onto the second book. The second book fell onto the third, and so on, until the last book hit the other bookend at the edge of the shelf.

The eye moved ahead to watch the bookend wobble off the shelf.

Jake's jaw dropped as the bookend plummeted through the air and onto Darryl's head.

Immediately, Darryl's mouth popped open to let out a yelp of pain and surprise that Jake could not hear. After all, it was his lone eye in the room, not his ear.

Darryl clutched his head in agony.

Jake's eye swooped in lower for a better view. It could see a trickle of blood seep between Darryl's fingers. No matter how hard Jake wanted to turn away, he couldn't help seeing through his other eye. At least he couldn't hear.

Then, Darryl's expression changed. Jake immediately knew why. Darryl was staring in the eye's direction.

For a second, it seemed as if Darryl had forgotten all about the pain. Now he was overcome with shock and horror.

The eye hung in the air, watching him.

Darryl pushed himself back against his bed, and then ran out of room, slamming the door shut behind him.

The eye picked up a new gleam of light coming from the hallway. A second later, the door flew open, throwing light into the room. The silhouettes of Darryl's parents came barging in.

The eye dropped to ground level before it could be spotted, slipped out the door, and floated down the hall.

Back in the bathroom, Jake let out a long, shaky sigh.

He'd heard of people getting concussions from solid blows to the head. How heavy was that bookend? Was Darryl all right? There'd been blood.

But there was nothing he could do now. The eye seemed to have a will of its own.

Maybe it was following Jake's deepest thoughts. Maybe it was controlling itself.

It occurred to Jake that he hadn't told his parents about any of this. But how could he? They'd see him with his empty eye socket and freak out, rush him to the hospital, and what would the doctors do? Crazy glue his eye back into his head?

Not if he didn't have his other eye. Not yet. Last night, the eye had come back to him in his sleep.

Jake trudged out of the bathroom, across the hall, and

quietly slipped into his room. He flopped onto the bed. All he could do was wait.

No. There was something he needed to do first.

He got out of bed, tiptoed to the window, and cracked it open. He pulled the screen open. A cool breeze spilled into the room.

Jake went back to his bed and pulled the covers up. He closed his eye and waited. He could see the other eye leaving the Richter home, making its way down the street. He'd been asleep and dreaming when it had returned to him the other night. Now he was wide awake. He wasn't sure what it would feel like to have his eye slip back into his own socket. He didn't really want to know what that was going to feel like, but he was going to find out.

Or was he?

Jake narrowed the eye still left in his head.

The eye wasn't heading back home. It was following a different route now.

Jake sat up in bed and closed his eye so he could focus on the other one.

He watched the eye track a new path through the suburbs. Where was it going? Why wasn't it coming back?

Jake sat up in bed and shivered.

He opened the eye that was still in his head.

Wherever it was headed, Jake had to stop it!

CHAPTER 6

It was already pushing three o'clock in the morning, but that didn't matter.

Jake quietly slipped on a pair of pants and a shirt and crept out to the backyard for his bike. It was a good thing he'd put the bike in the backyard instead of the garage. Opening the garage door at this hour would wake his parents up, and probably the neighbours too.

He tiptoed to the shed in the back of the garden. Jake was relieved to find the door unlocked. He dug into his pocket for a penlight and shone it around. Rope. He'd need rope to help him on this mission. Jake had a feeling the eye might be hard to catch, and he might need to climb something in order to get to the eye — like up on a roof, or the second storey of a building.

It was a good thing his parents kept the shed stocked with all manner of garden gear, including a good length of rope. Jake took it off the hook and threw the coil over his neck. Then, back to the bike.

He pedalled fast, but it wasn't easy trying to stay balanced on the bicycle. Not only was his depth perception shot, but his mind was also struggling to process two separate moving images from both eyes.

It's kind of like being a chameleon, Jake thought. Those bug-catchers had a pair of eyes that could rotate independently of one another to give the lizard two different views of the world around it.

But a chameleon's eyes were attached to a body that moved at one speed. Jake's disembodied eye was moving at a different speed than he was on the bike. His head soon ached from the strain of having to make sense of two images at once. He wanted to stop and take a break, but there wasn't time for that.

The good news was that at least the eye wasn't far away. He could recognize the street signs, and knew how to follow the eye. Jake took a shortcut, blazed like lightning down a side street, and rounded a corner.

Jake tried to take it as quickly as the eye had, and nearly flew over the handlebars. He hit the brakes and burned a layer of rubber off on the road.

The back tire pushed forward, and Jake had to plant his feet to keep from pitching off the bike.

There it was, illuminated under a streetlight half a block away.

At first it looked like one of the many moths clustering around the streetlight. But the eye was not drawn to the light, and it didn't flap wings. It just hovered there, in the air.

Jake could see everything the eye saw. He stood frozen on his bike, watching himself watch himself. The two images bled together. It was hard to separate them. Humans weren't meant to see this way.

Then the eye turned and pushed back into the night.

Jake let out a groan and pedalled on.

It was almost as if the eye wanted Jake to follow it.

Why else would it keep to the streets? Why else would it stop to let him catch up?

Jake sped on. The road dropped down to a hill, and Jake pedalled as if his life depended on it. The bike raced down the street, picking up as much speed as a car might. The wind tore at his hair and whipped his shirt into ruffles. He squinted his empty eye socket closed and held out his hand. His fingertips were just inches away from the white orb that belonged back in his skull.

He almost had it. Just a few inches more—

The eye swerved out of the way.

It was playing with him.

And Jake knew where it was leading him.

Back to the cemetery.

Jake's head was full of questions, but the biggest one still wasn't answered.

Why?

The question was still throbbing in his head as he pedalled his bike to the front gates of the cemetery. The eye pushed ahead, flying between the bars of the cemetery gates, over the tombstones, and toward the drop-off that led to the other cemetery. The one people weren't meant to visit.

Jake screeched to a halt.

The eye had easily passed through the cemetery gates; the rest of Jake's body was another matter. He was too bulky to fit through. This meant he'd have to climb, hence the rope.

It took a few tries to toss the rope over one of the larger branches on the tree, but once the rope was secure, the rest was relatively easy. Jake took both ends and wrapped them around the palms of his hand. Then he pulled himself up along the edge of the cemetery wall. Once over the edge, Jake lowered himself down and retrieved the rope. He'd need that to keep from slipping down the hill to the other cemetery.

Jake was alone in the cemetery.

The tombstones stood guard, the dead still buried beneath them. Jake felt a twinge of unease. It was like he was being watched.

That was just it, *he was*.

Jake closed his eye, and the image he received made his skin crawl.

It was an image of himself in the cemetery, seen from a distance. But the distance was shortened as the eye moved in closer. It had been waiting for him. It knew he would follow. Could it see the things he saw with his other eye?

Soon, the eye was just a few feet from Jake's other, closed eye. He opened it and gasped.

He hadn't seen his own eye before. Not like this, floating a few feet from his face, staring back at him.

The sensation of looking at the floating eye *and* seeing himself through it was a bit much. The two images overlapped in his mind, almost as one.

Then the eye moved away.

Jake didn't need to ask. The eye clearly wanted him to follow.

Coiling the rope over his shoulder, Jake dug into his pocket for the penlight and switched it on. At first he trained the beam right on the eye itself, but that just made one of the images in his mind too bright, and he had to squint. Instead, he positioned the penlight beam on the ground, a few feet to the side of the eye.

Soon the ground dropped away to reveal the steep hill. Down below, all Jake could see were treetops and pooling shadows.

Jake tied the end of the rope to a nearby tree and lowered himself down to the bottom. The eye was waiting for him there.

Jake followed it through the woods to the other cemetery. The eye stopped when it reached the bald spot in the forest with the tombstone covered in dead weeds.

The eye looked at Jake. Let's face it: that was all the eye could do. It was an expressionless thing. There was a lot you could read into a person's eyes when they were in their sockets: a face could move eyebrows, close eyelids, blink. But detached from a human face, all an eye could do was stare. There was no way to read any emotion. The eye was just a lone organ from his body in the wrong place.

There was more to it than that, though. The eye was able to move and focus on things. The pupil dilated when it was interested in something. Maybe it couldn't express itself, but there was thinking going on, not from the eye itself, but from whoever or whatever was controlling it. Some of that thinking came from Jake. Some of it came from somewhere else.

Once again, Jake was overcome with a creeping sensation. The hairs on his skin prickled. His mouth went dry. His heart thumped like a drum solo.

The eye turned away and hovered near one of the two sharp tips on top of the tombstone. It weaved in and around the spikes, as if daring Jake to come close and snatch it.

Jake hesitated. It was like trying to catch a fly with one's hands. Jake just needed to wait for the right moment, and then grab it. But the eye was fast. And smart. It hovered there, waiting for him, like the thing had a brain. Jake held his ground, thinking about when to make his move.

How much longer could he wait? If he didn't catch the eye now, who knew where it would fly off to next?

Jake kept staring at the eye, and the eye stared back. He was picturing two different views of himself regarding ... *himself*, and shuddered. What was the eye thinking? Was it waiting? If so, waiting for what?

Jake didn't want to find out. He shot out his hand to snatch the eye.

"Yee-ouch!" Jake yelped, and retracted his hand.

He'd done it again. This time, it was his hand that had gotten scratched against the jagged edge of the spiky bit on the tombstone.

Jake clutched his arm to his chest and waited for the stinging sensation to go away. Was the cut deep? He held his breath and looked down. Blood seeped from the wound at the back of his hand. He'd had worse cuts and scrapes, but this one troubled him.

It was as if the eye had *wanted* him to scrape his hand. The spiky end of the tombstone was what had got him here in the first place.

Sure enough, now that he'd scratched his hand, the eye hovered back to Jake, almost nestling itself in Jake's bloody palm. Jake curled his fingers around the eye. The eye didn't even try to escape. Now it simply stared up at him.

It had lured him back here. Jake was sure of it. The question was, *why?*

Inspecting the stone more closely, Jake saw that there was something unnatural about it. Some tombstones had polished stone surfaces; there were plenty examples of those in the other cemetery. But this stone was almost metallic. Jake brushed his hand along the surface, and his fingertips tingled, as if the thing were electric. He gave the stone a hard knock.

There was no inscription on the stone. Only a blank surface.

No, Jake thought. There was something there, still covered with weeds. Jake pulled them away and fixed the penlight on a small section of the tombstone.

S.C., it read.

Jake narrowed his eye. The writing looked as if it had been scratched into the stone with a knife, like graffiti.

What did the letters mean?

Jake had seen two such letters before, in the word "SCRUMB" that was carved into Jonathan's desk in Mr. Glick's class.

All of a sudden, it hit Jake. The letters had been written in precisely the same way. It was the same hand that had carved them both, and Jake now knew what the letters were.

They were initials!

S.C., Jake understood, but now he had a last name to go along with it. "SCRUMB" was really "S. Crumb," whoever that was.

Was S. Crumb the person buried under this tombstone? Was it the person controlling his eye?

The eye still lay in his hand. It felt like a lump of cold jelly. An oversized grape he dare not crush.

The eye was far too dirty to put back in his empty socket. Instead, Jake slipped the eye in the pocket on his shirt and buttoned it shut for safekeeping.

It was nearly five o'clock in the morning by the time Jake returned, exhausted, to his house, and snuck inside. He tip-toed up the creaky stairs, slipped into his bedroom, changed back into his pajamas, and threw his dirty clothes in the hamper. He could explain those later. Now he needed a little shut-eye. Both eyes, in fact.

Before heading back to sleep, Jake took his eye to the bathroom. The eye had brushed against all the dirt by the tombstone, which meant he'd have to clean it.

He turned the tap on and adjusted the faucet to a comfortable temperature. Then he lowered his hand under the tap. He flinched at the feeling of the water running over his naked eye. Jake had always hated eye drops, and this was far worse.

When the last specks of dirt were gone, Jake took the eye and brought it back to his face. He turned the pupil away from the empty socket and pointed it at the mirror. Staring at himself, the two images in his mind lined up again. What a relief it was to be seeing the way he was used to. Jake stretched the muscles around his eye socket and pushed ...

The eye popped back into place, like a piece in a jigsaw puzzle.

Jake rubbed his eye, blinked, and stared at his reflection.

It was almost time to get whatever little sleep he could before school. There was only one thing left to do.

Jake pulled open a drawer under the sink and found a roll of tape. He pulled off a few pieces and fixed his eye shut.

"Be a good eye, and *stay!*"

CHAPTER 7

"What are you doing with tape on your face?"

Groggily, Jake blinked himself awake. His mother stood over him, frowning.

There was only one image in his mind, which meant that both eyes were in his head. Come to think of it, if they hadn't been, the look on his mother's face would be quite different. Jake breathed a sigh of relief.

"I just wanted to make sure my eye was okay," he answered.

"Your eye is fine," his mother reassured him. "*You're* fine. Now go get dressed and eat some breakfast."

She left the room. Jake peeled back the covers and touched the tape with his fingers. He wasn't a fan of pulling off bandages. He was just about to get up to go to the bathroom to wet the tape, loosen the glue, when —

"YOW!"

Jake ripped the tape from his eye.

His mouth hung open, now more in shock than in pain. Why had he done that? It went against the system. Jake never went against the system.

61

He rubbed the skin around his eye, and grew aware of a painful sensation in his hand. Jake saw the deep gash along the side of his hand where he'd grazed the protruding edge of the tombstone. It was painful, yes, but also … itchy, like a healing scab.

Jake lowered his hand. He drummed his fingers against the bedside table. It wasn't the sort of thing he was used to doing, but moving his fingers like that made him ignore the itch.

First the eye, now *this*. Jake hobbled out of bed and scratched his hand. He'd barely gotten any sleep, and was probably just acting funny.

Once he got past the fact that he possessed a floating eye with a mind of its own, nothing seemed out of the ordinary.

Except …

While eating his morning cereal, Jake kept pushing down on his spoon to turn it into a catapult.

While brushing his teeth, Jake flicked his pasty toothbrush at the mirror, covering it in little white speckles.

It was only when he got to school that things seemed to get — how should he say it — *out of hand*.

To begin with, Darryl Richter showed up with a black eye and a nasty cut on the side of his head. Jake didn't know whether to shiver or breathe a sigh of relief. The dream had been real, but at least Darryl hadn't been hurt so badly that he needed to stay in the hospital.

Darryl definitely looked spooked. He hung back by the far fence, huddled around Horace and Malcolm.

"Looks like Richter got what was coming to him!" Jonathan smiled gleefully from the paved tarmac. "I wish I could find whoever did that and shake his hand," Jonathan added.

Shake his hand? Jake's hand was shaking pretty badly now, and it had nothing to do with Darryl Richter!

Jake stared in Darryl's direction, feeling the guilt well up inside him. The eye could have done some real damage, more than giving Darryl a black eye.

It could have even *killed* him.

"You tired or something?" Jonathan asked.

Jake shrugged.

"Darryl Richter got the heck knocked out of him, and you aren't going to celebrate?"

"He looks hurt," Jake managed, his voice shaking. If Jonathan only knew ...

Jonathan shook his head. "We're talking about Darryl Richter, the guy who nearly flattened you at the cemetery."

Jake flashed Jonathan a look that caused his friend to back away.

"Whoa!"

"Whoa, what?"

"Dude, you just gave me ... the evil eye."

Jake flashed Jonathan another look.

"There. You did it again."

"What are you talking about?"

"Don't you see it?"

"See what?"

"One of your eyes is moving differently than the other. How did you do that?"

Jake's heart raced. He needed to tell somebody about what was happening, but not here. Not now.

"It's just feeling a bit ... twitchy," Jake said.

It was true. He did feel twitchy, but not so much in his eye right now. The twitching came from his hand, the left

63

hand that had been injured. He couldn't stop moving its fingers.

Jonathan was quick to notice. "Are you doing air piano or something?"

Jake clenched his left hand into a fist.

"All right, all right," Jonathan said. "No need to get angry."

"I'm not angry."

"Your fist is so tight that your knuckles look like they're about to come through your skin," Jonathan noted.

Jake looked down. The left hand had squeezed into the tightest fist he'd ever seen. Jake's knuckles were white. The veins on his hand bulged. His whole arm was shaking.

"That's weird," Jake said.

Jonathan nodded. Things had been weird with Jake for the last few days. Of the two of them, it was usually Jonathan who did weird things.

"By the way," Jake started, "I figured out what that word 'scrumb' means. It's really somebody's name: S. Crumb."

"That makes sense," Jonathan agreed. "What made you think of that?"

Jake didn't answer at first. When was he going to tell Jonathan about what had happened at the cemetery? "It just came to me," he lied.

Jonathan's eyes lit up. "I bet you this S. Crumb's a student at school then, right?"

"Right," Jake nodded. "But there aren't any kids named Crumb here."

"So he or she is an older student, then. Somebody who graduated a long time ago, maybe."

"How do we find this Crumb kid, then? Assuming he's

a kid."

Jonathan narrowed his eyes. "Why's it so important?"

Jake's hand shook with a sudden spasm. His fingers stiffened into a talon-like pose, pointing straight at Jonathan's throat.

"Whoa! Jake! Chill out, it was just a question."

Jake massaged his fingers back into a normal position. "Sorry. I … I didn't sleep much last night. I'm just feeling a bit off."

"I'll say," Jonathan noted. It was time to change the subject. "Wanna come stare at Darryl Richter with me?"

Jonathan stopped Jake on their way into class. He tugged on Jake's coat sleeve and pointed up at the wall. "Look!"

Jake shook his head. "What am I supposed to be looking at?"

"Don't you see it? There it is!"

Jake looked at the wall above the Grade 2 coat racks. There were some old pictures of graduating classes from what seemed like a lifetime ago. The pictures were in black and white, and quite faded. They were all made up of small, labelled headshots of Grade 8 students. Jake had never bothered to pay them any attention before, but Jonathan's eyes were bugging out of his head. He jumped up and down.

"It's him! Crumb!"

Jonathan pointed to one of the pictures of the graduating class. There, right near the top right hand corner, was a small picture of a boy, and underneath the words "Shawn Crumb."

Jake shivered. So this was the mysterious S. Crumb. He had something to do with all of this, Jake was sure of it. But what?

At least they knew his name now.

Jake sensed a presence behind him and turned around. Mr. Glick was standing over both boys, his eyes also on the picture of the graduating class. "Class of '54," Mr. Glick started. "My grandfather taught those students. Things sure were different in those days," he mused. "Back then, if a student misbehaved, they'd get the strap."

Jonathan and Jake gulped audibly.

Mr. Glick smiled. "Thankfully, we've gotten rid of that barbaric practice. Why don't you two go hang your coats up and get ready for class?"

Jonathan and Jake hurried along their way. Once their coats were hung and their books had been taken out of their bags, they shuffled into the classroom with the rest of the students.

Today, the class was strangely quiet. Most people were trying not to stare at Darryl Richter's black eye. Nobody was asking the big question, like how could Darryl Richter, of all people, wind up with a black eye?

A weird tension filled the room. Normally, Darryl would cut it with some tough comment, like how he was going to spit in Jake's sandwich, but Darryl didn't make eye contact with anybody. He took out a book and sat quietly at his desk. Jake could have sworn that Darryl looked worried, an emotion he had never seen on the thug before.

The class didn't have long to stare or gawk. Today was Friday, and that meant a spelling dictation right after bell work.

In all of the craziness of the week, Jake had completely forgotten to study the words. He sat there trying to figure out the increasingly challenging word list.

"Enunciate," Mr. Glick enunciated. Then he placed the word into a sentence. "Listen to me enunciate the word enunciate."

Jake clenched his fingers. Stupid spelling. Stupid dictation! *Stupid everything!*

The pencil in his hand snapped.

A few of the students around him raised their heads as Jake inspected the broken pencil. He raised his hand to catch Mr. Glick's attention.

"What is it, Jake?"

"My pencil, uh, broke."

Mr. Glick nodded. "Go get a new one."

Jake did so quickly. He fished a fresh one out of the box from Mr. Glick's desk and put it into the pencil sharpener. The pencil sharpener sounded like the spinning turbine of a jet engine. Jake ground the pencil down to a fine point, pulled it out, and felt the tip. Perfectly pointy. He smiled to himself, then noticed that Mr. Glick — and the rest of the class — were staring in his direction.

"Sorry," he said, his smile fading, and walked back to his desk.

Once seated, Mr. Glick continued with the dictation.

"Articulate," he pressed on. "Listen to me *articulate* the word enunciate."

Man, those spelling words were hard.

Snap!

Horace Hobart and three or four other students seated around Jake turned to see him holding another freshly broken pencil in his hand. So did Mr. Glick, who was now looking at Jake with a curious expression on his face. "Is something the matter?"

Jake could only stare helplessly at the pencil in his hand. He shook his head. "I'm sorry. I can still use it."

Mr. Glick was just about to read the next word when Jake forced his thumb against the tip of the pencil, snapping it off.

"Interrupt," Mr. Glick orated from the front of the class. "I can *interrupt* a spelling dictation by breaking my pencil."

Jake ignored the chuckles bubbling around him. He was too busy staring at the pencil, and the twitching hand that clutched it. Now he couldn't even write with the thing. Unless he got up out of his desk, went to the sharpener, and broke everyone's concentration again.

"Embarrassed," Mr. Glick pressed on. "I was *embarrassed* when I interrupted the spelling dictation."

Jake tapped Lindsay on the shoulder. "Psst."

Lindsay whipped around. "What?" Her eyes registered annoyance.

"Can I borrow your sharpener?"

Lindsay grumbled, reached into her desk, and slammed the hand-held pencil sharpener on Jake's desk. He jammed the pencil into the sharpener and twisted it. All the while, Jake sat there listening to Mr. Glick read out more words he couldn't write down.

Two broken pencils in the span of five minutes. Jake had gained a violent streak this morning.

He felt his fingers twist against plastic and looked down. His desk was littered with wooden shavings. He'd gone and sharpened the entire pencil, right up to the metal end with the eraser. Jake pulled the pencil out and held it between his thumb and index fingertip. How was he going to write with this?

"Nice work, wimposaurus."

Jake's eye flared. It turned in its socket to stare at Horace Hobart, busy trying to stifle a laugh.

That did it.

Jake picked up the pencil sharpener, along with a big handful of pencil shavings. In one strong thrust, he hurled the contents of his hand at Horace Hobart.

"Ow!"

Mr. Glick looked up from the list of spelling words in his hand to find Horace Hobart covered in pencil shavings and rubbing the side of his head. Hobart was turned to Jake, a look of disbelief on his face. Jake's left hand had formed a fist that he shook in Horace's direction. All eyes in the class had turned to the boys.

Mouths dropped. Gasps were heard.

Horace's lower lip wobbled. He looked on the verge of tears, but somehow found it in him to convert crying to rage. His face went red, and he jabbed a finger in Jake's direction. "Jake threw pencil shavings at me!"

The class erupted into laughter.

Mr. Glick strode forward so that he was standing over Jake. "Office."

Jake shrunk back into his chair. "But it was an accident ..."

"*Now.*"

Under normal circumstances, Jake would have obeyed his teacher. Up until now, the two had gotten along just fine.

What Jake did next took him entirely by surprise. It took the entire class by surprise. Most surprised of all was Mr. Glick. But it wasn't the sort of surprise he wanted to receive.

The surprise was a finger.
Jake gave it to Mr. Glick.
It wasn't the right finger to give.

Chapter 8

"Suspended?!"

"That's what I said."

"Suspended?!" Jonathan raised his voice so loudly that it was likely the whole neighbourhood could hear. "You are so dangerous, dude! Plus, think of all the TV you'll get to watch at home."

Jonathan always tried to see the bright side of things.

Jake narrowed his eyes. "It's not an at-home suspension. I'm going to be stuck working in the office tomorrow."

Jonathan stopped in his tracks. "Why are we walking to my place?" Jonathan asked. "Your mom will know you're late. She'll get even angrier and punish you more."

"The punishment doesn't matter," Jake said.

Only when they reached Jonathan's house and snuck upstairs to his bedroom did Jake decide to come clean about everything that had been going on for the last few days.

"There's something wrong with my eye," Jake admitted.

"Yeah, I saw."

"But it's more than that."

"Do you have pink eye or something? Make sure you

wash your hands, I don't want to get infected." Jonathan immediately flung open a desk drawer to produce a bottle of hand sanitizer. He squirted a thick wad into his hands and started rubbing them together. The room filled up with the smell.

"I don't have pink eye," Jake returned.

"Well, that's a waste of good hand sanitizer."

"I have ..." Jake thought about what Jonathan had described earlier in the schoolyard. "I have, uh, Evil Eye." Jake thought about this a moment longer. "And an Evil Hand."

Jonathan looked confused.

"As in, my eye and hand, are ... well ... evil."

"Evil how?"

How could he show Jonathan? Maybe if he concentrated on something to follow. Jake searched about the room and saw Jonathan's prized collection of horror movie action figures. He stared at them intently.

"Why are you staring at my action figures?"

"Don't interrupt me. I'm concentrating."

Focus. *Focus*, he told himself. It wasn't working. His hand kept tapping on the table, disturbing his concentration. It clearly didn't want Jake's eye to leave his skull, or so Jake thought. He couldn't make the eye come out of his head. That only seemed to happen in dreams, when his mind was given to wandering. There was only one other option Jake had left.

"Promise me you're not going to tell anyone about what I'm going to do," Jake told Jonathan.

"Why?"

"Because it's really weird. And gross."

"Weird and gross is good," Jonathan smiled, nodding

enthusiastically. Then he saw the look on Jake's face and waved him off. "All right, all right. I promise not to tell."

"Okay. Take my hand."

"Which one?"

"The bad one," Jake said, and pointed to the hand that was still tapping on the desk.

"You've got to stop doing that with your hand, it's really annoying."

"I can't help it," Jake admitted. "But I have the feeling my hand is going to try to stop me from doing what I'm about to do. Do you have any rope or string?"

Jonathan opened up another desk drawer and fished out a length of twine.

"Good. Now cut it and tie my bad hand to the side of the chair."

Jonathan smiled. "This is getting weird already. I like it!"

He wrapped the twine around the hand at the wrist, and knotted it tight. The pressure cutting against Jake's circulation made him wince, but if the hand was going to struggle, let it feel pain. Even if Jake was on the receiving end of that pain.

"Now tie it to the chair," Jake instructed.

Jonathan made a move to do so.

The hand sprang to life. It yanked Jake's arm toward Jonathan's neck. Fingers clamped around Jonathan's throat and squeezed. Hard.

"Jake —" Jonathan was cut short and now struggling for air.

Jake grabbed hold of his forearm and yanked it back, but the fingers had taken on a life of their own, pressing down

73

hard against Jonathan's neck. He could feel the weight of his hand squeeze the jugular vein, and feel Jonathan's pulse quicken.

"No!" Jake blurted.

It was a stupid idea to even think about tricking the hand. Jonathan's face was going red. His eyes bulged in their sockets. How much longer did he have?

Jake did the only thing he could think of doing. He reached into Jonathan's desk, grabbed a pair of scissors, and jabbed the back of his possessed hand.

Immediately, the hand loosened its grip, the fingers flailing in a pain that Jake could also feel. A few drops of blood splashed against the floor. Jake bit hard, trying not to scream out.

Jake wrenched his evil hand away from Jonathan, who sat heaving for air. He rubbed his neck, now ringed with red, and tried to breathe. Once he'd breathed some life back into himself, and once Jake had control of the hand, Jonathan slid his chair closer to Jake. He took hold of the string and yanked the hand down. Jake let out a yelp of pain, but Jonathan was already at work knotting the other end of the twine to the chair. He'd learned how to tie knots at summer camp, and got the job done in seconds. Then he pushed his chair back away from Jake and stared at his best friend, one wriggling hand tied to the chair.

"What the heck do you think you're doing?!" Jonathan barked when he had a moment.

"I told you, my hand is evil."

"If this is some kind of joke, it's not funny. You could have killed me." He shifted his attention to Jake's hand tied to the chair. It was trying to stretch the fingers back to undo the knot, but to no avail. Jonathan was good with knots.

"I'm sorry," Jake breathed, feeling shaky.

"What? For almost killing me?"

"That, and for the next part," he continued.

He had to be delicate with this next bit. It was hard to keep one hand steady while the other was busy trying to tear itself free from the chair.

Jake swallowed, raised his hand to his head, extended his thumb and index finger, and reached for his eye.

Jonathan looked like he was going to be sick. "What are you doing?"

"Watch."

Jake dug his finger into his eye socket. It slipped into the tight space behind Jake's eye.

Jonathan's mouth dropped open. "That's disgusting!"

Jake jammed his finger further into the socket, right behind his eyeball, and popped it out. It fell onto the table and rolled to a stop, so that it was staring right up at Jonathan.

Jonathan took a second to regard the eye. Lying there on the table, it didn't appear too unusual. He'd seen fake eyes before. Then he turned his attention to Jake's face. He saw the empty socket, looked back at the gooey eye on the desk, and turned around to puke into his garbage can.

Jake was waiting for him when he'd wiped his mouth clean. "I thought you liked gory movies," Jake said.

"You ... you just popped your eye right out of your head."

"Yes."

"That's, like, medically impossible."

"Yes. And so is this," Jake said. He pointed back to the table. The eye lifted away, floating in the air. It traced a path back to Jonathan's eye socket and fit itself back in. Clearly it did not want to be used right now.

Jonathan turned away and threw up again. When he wiped his mouth clean, he reached into the desk drawer for some minty chewing gum. "How did you do that?"

"It had something to do with that tombstone," Jake said. "I can sort of control it, like when I concentrate really hard, or if I get a strong feeling. But I don't know how to stop it. And there's something else."

"Yeah, I'll say."

Jake shook his head. "No, you don't understand, Jonathan. It's not just me that's controlling it. That's why my hand tried to kill you just then. I need your help."

Jonathan threw his hands in the air. "How am I supposed to help?"

Jake waved around the room with his free hand. "Look at this place!" he exclaimed. There were all sorts of ghoulish horror posters tacked to the wall. His shelves were overflowing with monster movie figurines, shrunken heads, fake gore. Jake wondered how Jonathan's parents let him keep all this stuff, but that didn't matter now. Jonathan was the best and only expert Jake knew he could share his secret with.

"Yeah, but it's not real," Jonathan retorted.

"Help me," Jake pleaded, his eyes going red with tears.

Jonathan let out a frustrated breath. "All right," he muttered. "I don't know what I can do, though."

"Have you ever seen anything like this before?"

Jonathan leaned forward in the chair, face planted in his hands, staring at Jake's still-twitching hand. "There are a bunch of old monster movies about disembodied hands. You've got *The Hands of Orlac*, *The Beast With Five Fingers*, a sequence from *Dr. Terror's House of Horrors*, *The Addams Family*, even a movie called *The Hand*. But your hand isn't disembodied ..." Jonathan looked up and pointed at Jake's face. "It's your eye that's disembodied."

"Both of them touched that tombstone in the other cemetery," Jake said. He explained about what happened with his eye going after Darryl Richter.

Jonathan couldn't suppress a laugh. "So *you* were the one who gave Richter the black eye! An eye for an eye, huh?"

"This is serious," Jake hissed. "I don't want anyone else getting hurt." Jake thought about this for a second. "I mean, now that you know about my secret, what if the eye comes after you?"

That seemed to shut Jonathan up. He sat there for a moment, then reached under his bed and pulled out a tennis racket. He swiped it through the air. "I'll be ready if it does." Jonathan's eyes went wide. "Hang on a sec. I've got an idea."

Jonathan swung around on his chair and started typing at his desktop computer. Jake watched as he sifted through his pictures, bringing up the ones he took at the other cemetery. "Maybe we can find some clues here," he muttered.

As Jake sat watching the pictures scroll by, he felt the eye twitch in its socket.

"Jonathan ..."

Jonathan was too busy scanning the pictures. He soon reached a picture of Jake standing over the lone tombstone.

"Jonathan ..."

"I know, I found the picture," he said.

"Don't puke," Jake said.

"Why?"

"Turn around."

77

Jonathan turned around. He was staring eye to eye ... with the eye.

Jonathan jumped.

"I thought you said you could only do that when you were sleeping."

"The eye can see the pictures," Jake said. "Maybe it wants to tell us something."

"It's an eye. It can't tell you anyth—" Jonathan stopped himself in mid-thought. He reached onto his desk and grabbed the scissors, a pad of paper, and a pen. "Dude, we've been going about this all wrong. Now, I'm going to free your hand, if you promise you won't try to strangle me."

Jonathan looked at the eye, made a bright smile, motioned with the scissors to the string tying the hand to the chair, and nodded hopefully.

The eye looked to Jake. Although it had no eyelids, Jake had the feeling it was winking at him.

So far, the hand had not attacked.

Jake rubbed his tender wrist. Jonathan passed him the pencil and pen. "What do I need these for?"

"If my hunch is right, your hand and eye are working together. Like partners. Now get your eye to look this way."

Jonathan opened a window on his computer and turned on his word processing program. He typed in a few words: CAN YOU READ THIS? IF SO, PLEASE SAY YES.

"Why are you writing in capitals? It looks like you're shouting."

But before Jonathan could answer, Jake's hand clutched the pen and scribbled something down on the page. Jake didn't use that hand for writing, but the hand gripped the pen properly. Jake looked down at what the hand had scribbled.

Yes, the hand had written.

Jake gasped.

"Awesome!" Jonathan exclaimed. "Now let's find out what this thing wants."

He typed some more: WHAT DO YOU WANT?

No sooner than Jake's eye had tracked Jonathan's typing than the hand sprang to action. Jake watched in amazement as the hand scribbled out some more: *Need the core.*

Jake looked up at Jonathan and narrowed his eyes. "I don't know what that means. What's the core?"

Jonathan shrugged.

WHAT'S THE CORE? he typed.

Need the core. Need the core. Need the core.

Jonathan rubbed his wrist as the hand finished writing. He wasn't used to using those hand muscles for writing, and it ached a bit.

"All right, so we need this core thingy. I'm guessing it has something to do with the tombstone."

Jonathan turned around to face Jake. "Any idea where the core might be?"

Jake's eyes lit up. "There was that name on the tombstone. S.C. — Shawn Crumb!"

"Right." Jonathan nodded, and turned back to start typing again.

WHO IS SHAW

Jake grabbed hold of Jonathan's arm and shoved it away from the keyboard.

"What are you doing?" Jonathan asked.

"Let's not give it too much information. Maybe it

doesn't know who … S. C. is."

Jonathan glanced at the eye. It had been tracking their conversation, moving its focus from Jake to Jonathan.

"Good point," Jonathan noted. "Do you think it can read lips?"

Jake shrugged. "If it did, it wouldn't need us writing things down for it."

"Nice. So we can probably talk about Crumb then, right?"

Jake looked at the eye. He covered his mouth with his good hand, so it couldn't read his lips … just in case.

"The eye may not know about Crumb. So let's keep it that way."

"Good point," Jonathan returned. "I've got one more question for this eye of yours."

Jonathan backspaced, then finished the question: WHAT IF WE CAN'T FIND THE CORE?

The eye looked from the computer, to Jonathan, and then to Jake.

Then the hand scribbled: *The boy will die.*

Once it had finished writing, the hand flung the pen to the ground, tightened up into a fist, and jammed itself into Jake's pocket.

Jake and Jonathan stared wordlessly at each other.

CHAPTER 9

If Jake was going to be grounded anyway for a) flipping the bird to Mr. Glick and b) not coming home after school, then he figured he might as well make the most out of it.

There had been initials scrawled on that tombstone in the middle of the not-cemetery: S.C. for Shawn Crumb. A quick search of the phone directory revealed that there was indeed one S. Crumb residing in town. Jake and Jonathan quickly went outside, grabbed their bikes, and pedalled their way over.

Crumb's house was in a shabby state. A layer of brick on the outer wall was in the process of slowly chipping off. An old, dried-up pine tree still stood in the front lot, more like a stone sentinel than a living, breathing thing.

"Maybe he is dead," Jonathan suggested, shaking his head at the state of the place.

Jonathan and Jake ran up the front porch, but stopped short of ringing the doorbell.

"We can't. This isn't right," Jake said.

"Sure it is." Jonathan stretched his arm out and rang the doorbell. Then he stuck his hands in his pockets and rocked back and forth on the balls of his feet. He started to whistle.

"This is a bad idea," Jake muttered.

"You don't like confronting problems," Jonathan snapped back. He smiled. "That's why you keep me around."

Jake opened his mouth to respond, but there wasn't any time. A figure appeared through the cracked frosted glass by the door. Metal latches clicked. The door slowly creaked open, and a withered face appeared in the narrow slit. It was a man's face. His cheeks were a patchwork of unshaven bits and razor burns. Despite a piercing stare, Jake noted that one of his eyes didn't track properly.

"Who are you?"

"I'm Jonathan, and this is Jake," Jonathan explained, as if this sort of answer was more than satisfactory.

"Yeah, yeah. *Kids.* I get that. You trying to sell me something? I don't want any of your Girl Scout cookies."

"Uh, we're boys," Jonathan noted.

"Girls, boys … I already bought your cookies."

"We're not selling cookies," Jake stated.

"Well, then what are you selling?"

"We're not selling anything. We've come to see Shawn Crumb —"

"Go away," the old man snapped, and slammed the door shut.

Jake and Jonathan stared at one another. "What crawled up his nostrils and died?" Jonathan asked.

Jake waved Jonathan off, and then stepped up to the door. Staring through the frosted glass beside the door, Jake could see that the old man was still in earshot. "Mr. Crumb, we came because of the tombstone. The one you carved your initials into —"

The door opened. Crumb's face popped out. "What do you know about *that?*"

Jake swallowed. "We're in a lot of trouble. We need to talk to you."

The old man looked at them. Still, one eye did not track properly. It just rested in its socket, staring out at the world lifelessly. It was like a doll's eye. Every time Crumb opened and closed his eyelids, the one eye just stared at them. No, *through* them. Like they weren't even there.

"You found the tombstone?"

"Yes."

"In the cemetery that isn't part of the regular cemetery?"

"Yes."

"Then why are you standing out there? Get inside before somebody sees you."

Jake wasn't sure about this. This Crumb was a stranger, and really weird-looking. Hadn't he been told a gazillion times about not taking rides with strangers? He was about to pull Jonathan over and whisper something about that in his ear, but Jonathan was already through the door.

Jake grumbled to himself and followed. Crumb slammed the door shut behind them.

The inside of Crumb's house was as shabby as Jake had predicted. It was a bungalow with a kitchen at the back, a living room in the front, and presumably a bedroom somewhere else in the midst of things. It smelled funny; a combination of stinky eggs and old laundry. The windows were caked with dirt, so that any sunlight streamed inside in mottled patches. The furniture was worn, and the wallpaper was faded and peeling. It was the sort of place you might be found dead in.

"Make yourself at home," Crumb snorted. He used a cane to hobble over to one of the chairs in the living room and plopped down. He stuck his hands into the pockets of his housecoat and stared at the two boys.

Jonathan and Jake sidled over towards the couch. Jonathan wrinkled his nose. "This place smells gross," he said.

Crumb took one hand out of his pocket, grabbed his cane, and jabbed it in the air in Jonathan's direction. "Sit down and shut yer trap!" he blurted.

Jonathan sat down. "I like this guy," he told Jake.

Jake had stopped listening. His hand was itchy again. Jake jammed the hand into his pocket. Did the hand or eye know anything about Shawn Crumb?

"Something wrong with your hand?" Crumb asked.

"Actually," Jonathan started, but Jake interrupted him before he could spill the beans.

"We found your name carved into that old tombstone," Jake said instead, very directly. He focused his eyes on Crumb.

"So you were saying."

"What do you know about that cemetery?" Jake asked.

"What makes you think it's a cemetery?" Crumb returned.

Jake felt a shiver run down his spine. "But it's full of tombstones …"

"Really? You see any names on those tombstones?"

"No."

Crumb leaned in closer. "You find any bodies buried under those tombstones?"

Jake turned to Jonathan. What was with this guy? They both shook their heads.

"What is it then?" Jake asked at last.

All Crumb did was shrug. "Darned if I know. I was a kid when I first came across the place. I'd been doing some research about our little town for a school project. Our grade school teacher wanted us to find out about the first settlers who came to Dundurn. Now, I was a pretty enthusiastic student. Not like you kids today, distracted by your colour television sets and digital watches and —"

"Hey," Jonathan spat. "I've never been distracted by a digital watch."

Crumb narrowed his eyes. "As I was saying, I was a bit of a keener. I wanted to do well on this project. Wanted to learn something of Dundurn's early history. So I found my way to the local library's special archive section. It was brimming with books and records that seemed hundreds of years old. I learned that the first settlers here included several families, including one Tobias Vaughan and family, Archibald Glick —"

Jake and Jonathan turned to one another. "Mr. Glick?" Jonathan erupted.

"See what I mean about distractible?"

"No, it's just that our teacher said his grandfather was buried in that cemetery," Jake returned. "Maybe that Archibald Glick was him."

Crumb shrugged. "Turns out that even I couldn't find some of those older tombstones. And with good reason. I came across some records from old journals from 1827. April 6, 1827, to be exact." Crumb stopped and looked at the boys, curious to see if that date meant anything to them. It didn't. Crumb crinkled his lips in annoyance and continued. "A shooting star was seen streaking through the sky. Some meteor fell to the ground with a huge bang. Windows were shattered across town. Many nearby buildings had severe structural damage. In fact, the central part of town was eventually relocated to where it is today."

"Why are you telling us this?" Jake asked.

Crumb shook his head. "You're not asking the right question," he said. "What you should be asking is: where did that meteor hit?"

Jake's eyes had gone wide. "The meteor hit the cemetery!" he exclaimed. "It probably also explains all the shattered bits of those old tombstones we found down there. That's why there's such a steep drop-off at the back. It's not a hill, it's a crater!"

Crumb nodded enthusiastically. "I'm glad to see someone put some brains in your head. I went down there and checked it out. It had been abandoned for quite some time. You could tell from all of the vegetation that was growing down there, even then. And you know what I found in the centre of that crater …"

"The tombstone," Jake whispered.

"The tombstone that isn't a tombstone," Crumb returned. "At first I thought it was a piece of rock from that meteorite."

Jake narrowed his eyes. "What do you mean, *at first?*"

"I don't think it was a meteorite that fell," Crumb continued. "At least, not at the speed that a regular meteorite falls."

"I don't understand."

"The meteorite should have been pulverized, right? Broken up into little bits. But that didn't happen. There are two spire-like protrusions extending from the edge of that hunk of rock."

"That is kind of weird," Jake admitted. "Maybe they're like, you know, stalactites, like from caves."

Crumb shook his head. "It would take thousands of years for them to form on either side of the stone like that. And what could cause it? Stalactites and stalagmites are formed by bits of minerals dripping down through water from cave walls. That rock's right out in the open."

Jonathan wasn't sure what to make of this. "Why didn't you tell anybody about your story, or what you found?"

Crumb shrugged. "I tried to. But too much stuff had grown over those tombstones to see them from the edge of the crater. Nobody believed my story or ideas. Even the kids my age laughed me off. But I wanted to leave some kind of clue, in case anyone did come across any more information. So I went and put my initials on that tombstone. I had to use the edge of my mother's old diamond ring; it was the only material that could scratch the stone. I figured if anyone ever did go down there and find those tombstones, they might one day come back to me. And if they did, I would warn them."

Jake felt his skin prickle. "Why?"

"You haven't touched the tombstone, have you?"

"Is touching the tombstone bad?"

Crumb leaned forward. He stared Jonathan in the eye. Then he stared Jake in the eye.

Jake's eye twitched.

Crumb's eye seemed to hold Jake's eye in its gaze. Jake's eye — the one that had been scratched by the tombstone — continued to twitch angrily in its socket.

"It's happened to you, hasn't it?"

"What do you mean?" Jake asked, not wanting to give

too much away, but why bother? He knew.

"First the voices. Wanting you to come closer. Wanting you to come so close you can touch it. But before you can, it does something to you. It made me fall. I cut my face on the tombstone. Scratched my eyeball," Crumb said.

Jake swallowed.

"Dreams came after that," he said. "Dark dreams. Seemed like I was following people that got on my nerves. Anger came after the dreams. I found out that my eye seemed to have a life of its own."

Jonathan nodded enthusiastically. "Yeah! That's exactly what's happened to Jake's eye. It's floating around, and ..." Jonathan's voice dropped. "But what about your eye, Mr. Crumb? I mean, it's just sitting there in your head. It can't even move."

"No. Not anymore."

"What do you mean, *not anymore?*"

Crumb took his finger and dug it into his eye socket, then popped out his eye. It fell into his palm and rolled around, like a lone marble.

Jonathan looked from the glass eye in Crumb's palm to the empty eye socket in his head and let out a yelp. He looked as if he was going to puke again.

"Glass eye," Crumb said. "The only one I can trust."

Jake was breathing harder now. "What do you mean, *trust?*"

"Well, that eye of mine started putting people in danger. So I had to get rid of it, didn't I? Had to make sure that whatever that tombstone wanted me to do couldn't happen." Crumb picked up the eye and wedged it back into its socket. He blinked a few times until the circle with the painted iris and pupil were facing outward. Then he stared straight at Jake. "That's what you're going to have to do, if you want this thing to stop."

Jake shook his head. Destroy his eye? Wasn't there another way to fix this? "I ... I can't ..."

Jonathan nudged Jake. "Go on. Tell him."

"Tell me what?" Crumb asked.

Jake pulled his hand out of his pocket. The fingers twitched spasmodically. "It got my hand, too," Jake said. "It said it was going to kill me if I didn't get it —"

"— the core," Crumb finished. His face went white. "It wants the core. After all these years, it's still active."

"How do you know?" Jonathan asked.

Crumb stood up. Jonathan and Jake hadn't been watching Crumb too carefully. At least, not all of him. If they had, they'd have noticed that Crumb also had been keeping one hand in his pocket. Now he pulled it out to reveal a prosthetic hand. It was a dull, waxy colour. "Seems like that tombstone is up to its old tricks again."

"Hang on a second!" Jonathan blurted. "It got your hand, too?"

Crumb nodded.

"It goes after the eyes and the hand," Jonathan said to himself. "So it can use a human to spy on things, pick up things ... like that core."

Jake just stared at the hand. "So, what happened to it?"

"Like I said, my eye was bad, so I got rid of it. My hand had the same problem. If you can excuse a pun, I took matters into my own hand."

Oh no. Jake felt like he was going to be sick. To get the voices out of his head, Crumb had amputated his own hand.

He'd obviously survived, but … "I can't cut my hand off," Jake said.

"Then I don't know what to tell you," Crumb returned.

"I need the core," Jake said. "Do you have it?"

Crumb's eyes momentarily widened. He stood up abruptly. "You need to go," he insisted. "I'm sorry I can't help you any more than I have. There's only one way to solve this problem. Go and find yourself a good surgeon."

"You know about the core," Jake snapped, getting to his feet.

Crumb shook his head. "The core won't solve your problems. It'll just make things worse."

"Where are you keeping it?"

"Safe," Crumb said, with more than a hint of finality.

"Please," Jake begged. "Just let us have the core."

Crumb shook his head. He pointed to the door with the hand that could still point.

Jake and Jonathan made their way to the front door.

"What do we do?" Jake asked Jonathan.

Jonathan whirled around to face Crumb. "Okay, we're going."

"Good. Go." Crumb replied.

Crumb had both hands out now. His real hand clutched the walking cane. The prosthetic hand hung limply at his side.

"I'm not leaving without a fist bump," Jonathan blurted.

"A what?"

Before Jonathan could explain, he turned his hand into a fist and made a move to bump it against Crumb's fake hand. At the last moment, Jonathan opened up his palm and grabbed hold of the prosthetic. Then he yanked.

"Gotcha!"

The hand popped out of Crumb's sleeve. "Yeargh!" Crumb exclaimed, clutching at the stump.

"What are you doing?!" Jake roared.

"Give it back!" Crumb reacted. He swung his cane viciously through the air. Jonathan jumped back. The cane smashed against the wall, leaving a dent.

"Give us the core and you'll get it," Jonathan returned. He looked at Jake and grinned. "See? I've always got ideas."

"That's my hand!" Crumb roared.

"Core," Jonathan stated, very firmly.

"Uh, Jonathan ..." Jake started.

But Jonathan was keeping his eyes locked on Crumb. Crumb's eyes were locked on the hand.

So were Jake's. "Jonathan," he said again.

"Not now, Jake. Can't you see I've got this situation well in hand?" He turned to Jake and grinned. "Good pun, eh?" He turned back to Crumb. "I mean, I've got to *hand* it to you, you put up a good fight. Now give us the core."

"Jonathan ..."

"What?!" Jonathan snapped, turning angrily to Jake. "I'm trying to help you out."

"You're holding the core."

"Huh?"

Jonathan looked down. Buried in the prosthetic hand itself was a conical piece of stone, smooth, like polished glass.

"Oh, wild," Jonathan said.

Smash!

The cane collided with the wall again, inches from Jonathan's face. Jonathan leapt back. Jake turned and opened the door.

Crumb came rushing after them, slicing the air with the cane.

Jonathan reached into the hand, yanked out the core, then tossed the hand back to him. "We're just borrowing it," he insisted.

"You don't know what you're doing!" Crumb shouted after them.

But Jake and Jonathan were already at the edge of the front lawn, getting back onto their bikes.

"Whatever you do, don't put the core into that stone!"

CHAPTER 10

"Suspended?!"

Jake's dad did not look pleased.

"It's only for a day," Jake said, as innocently as he could. He was sitting in the living room in a chair. Both of his parents stood over him, arms folded across their chests, their eyebrows creased and glowering.

"You never mentioned any problem with your teacher before," Jake's mother snapped. "Why did you do it?"

Why? It was his left hand. It had gone Bad with a capital B, and had threatened to *kill* Jake if he didn't bring it some crazy core. It wasn't the sort of story he could tell his parents.

Besides, now he *had* the core. He had to get to the cemetery to bring it to whatever was at that tombstone. That was the only thing that could make this all go away.

Or not. Shawn Crumb had warned him against it, but he also wanted Jake to chop his own hand off. As if.

Jake's left hand was going wild. His fingers were in constant motion now. The only way to keep it under control was to wedge his hand under his bum and hope that his own body weight would do the trick. Jake rocked back and forth on the chair, waiting for his parents to go away.

They didn't.

"And then instead of coming home to deal with the situation, you go sauntering off to Jonathan's. And out for a stroll afterwards?"

Jake opened his mouth to respond. What could he say? Neither his mother nor his father was in any mood to listen. They were just angry. Jake couldn't exactly blame them. His recent behaviour wasn't like him.

"I've never had to say this to you, Jake, but you're grounded."

Jake's eyes went wide. "Grounded?"

"Yes. As in, after you've served your in-school suspension tomorrow, you come right back here and you stay."

"For how long?"

Jake's dad turned to his mother. To Jake, it seemed like an invisible, telepathic conversation went between them. Jake's parents had an unusual way of silently communicating. Most of the time, it seemed as if Jake's dad was receiving orders from Jake's mom. But it was Jake's dad who always did the talking. And the punishment-doling.

Jake's dad turned from Jake's mom and stared sternly at his son. "Until we say so."

Jake's hand was going into spasms now. He had to figure out a way to contact Jonathan.

"Can I go now?"

"Go upstairs. No TV."

"Okay."

Jake jammed his hand into his pocket and scuttled out of the room. In any other situation, getting his parents this angry was liable to make him cry. Now he was too preoccupied with everything else to spill any tears.

Up the stairs he went, into his room, and closed the door behind him.

He heard a muffled conversation from downstairs: obviously his parents talking about the punishment, or groceries, or whatever.

At least they were talking. Now was the time to give Jonathan a shout. Jake had a phone in his room. He picked it up and held the receiver to his ear, then quickly punched in Jonathan's cell number.

Jonathan picked up in less than a ring.

"So, you grounded or what?" he said.

"Don't start," Jake breathed.

"Well, we've got to get to that cemetery, don't we?"

"Shawn Crumb warned us not to."

"Yeah. This coming from a guy who hacked off his own hand and wanted you to do the same."

"So what do we do?" Jake asked. "I can't leave. My parents will see."

"I know," Jonathan said. "That's why we're going to wait."

"Until when?"

"Midnight."

"Why midnight?"

"My parents usually conk out by eleven. How do you think I manage to watch all those late-night horror movies?"

"Okay," Jake replied. "Midnight it is."

"Meet me at the end of Elm Street. And bring your bike."

Midnight came.

Jake found his way out of the house, grabbed his bike, and walked it to the end of the road before pedalling over to Elm Street. How many times was he going to have to sneak out in the dead of night and break into the cemetery?

At least he had Jonathan for company this time.

It made breaking into the place a little easier, too. Someone could help pull the rope for the other person when scaling the wall. Now Jake and Jonathan shone their flashlights through the cemetery. The night air was crisp enough that their breath left little clouds of vapour. To Jake, the idea of sneaking out of his house against his parents' wishes, in the middle of the night, to break into a cemetery, was possibly the worst idea he could ever have thought of.

"This is the best thing we've ever done!" Jonathan exclaimed.

At least Jonathan was here. If they were going to get into trouble, it helped that a friend was along for the ride.

Silently, they made their way through the graveyard, down the hill, to the other cemetery.

They pressed on, moving through the woods and not stopping until they reached the tombstone in the circular bald spot.

They stood staring at the tombstone. Jake's fingers flickered. His eye twitched. "What now?"

Jonathan gave him the device. "I guess you put it in."

"Why me?"

"It's your eye and hand that got bit by that thing. Maybe putting the core in will fix everything."

"Not likely," Jake said, "but worth a shot."

Jake held the core in his palm. It was cold and heavy. Kind of a cool artifact, Jake thought to himself, but one he needed to get rid of.

The fingers on his left hand twitched with manic life. Hopefully this core business would do the trick, and Jake could have control of his hand again. He dropped to his knees and tore away at the weeds covering the tombstone. The weeds were so thick that even Jake's possessed hand couldn't do it alone. "Help me with this," Jake blurted to Jonathan.

Jonathan joined Jake to pick the tombstone clean of all weeds. After, they sat back and trained their flashlight beams on the tombstone, huffing from exhaustion.

"Look at that thing," Jonathan breathed, his face flushed, his skin soaked with sweat.

The tombstone was smooth as a piece of polished glass, save for the scratches that Shawn Crumb had carved into it and a hole in the direct centre of the stone.

Jake squeezed the core in his hand and then turned to the hole. No doubt the core would fit perfectly into the hole. Jake's hand twitched in anticipation. He sat up and hobbled over to the hole. Just shove the core in, and then —

Jake wrinkled his brow. And then what? How was he to guarantee that whatever force had taken over his eye and hand wouldn't want to take over anything else?

"I don't know about this," Jake whimpered. "Maybe we should go back. Or get someone to help us. Like our parents. Or even the police."

"Oh yeah," Jonathan snapped. "Get them to watch us break into a cemetery. We're on our own with this one, Jake."

Jonathan trained his flashlight beam on the hole. Jake let out a shaky sigh.

Fine. Let this end it. Let whatever was buried under the tombstone have the stupid core, and let it free Jake's hand

and eye. Just let this be over.

Jake lined the core up with the hole, and then slid it in.

Click.

The core formed a perfect match with the hole. Like the last missing piece of a jigsaw puzzle finally back in place.

Jake backed away from the tombstone.

Click. Click.

There was nothing left to click in place, but apparently nobody had told the tombstone that.

Cracks began to form in the stone. They radiated out from the centre around the core. Jake wondered if putting the core in had broken the tombstone, but a closer look at the cracks revealed something else. The cracks were forming geometric patterns and fissures in the stone.

Click–click–click …

Chunks of the tombstone swung open, as if they'd been sitting on hinges. But there were no hinges to this stone. Some force was pulling it apart bit by bit, tiny pieces at first, but soon opening more and more.

After a moment, enough of the stone bits had flipped to the sides to reveal a small part of the tombstone's interior. Jake shone his flashlight at it, but the hole was too small to get a good look inside.

The ground around them rumbled.

"Whoa! What's happening? An earthquake?"

The ground shook so heavily that Jake and Jonathan were thrown from their feet. Insects spilled out of the earth and scurried away. Centipedes and worms ran through Jake's fingers, and he pulled away in revulsion. Jonathan dropped his flashlight. It rolled off so the beam lit only a small corner of the tombstone. A swarm of moths blotted that out, too.

Jake staggered back. "What have we done?"

The lone beam of Jonathan's flashlight revealed something new. The tombstone began to rise from the ground, like the earth was spitting it up.

"Okay," Jonathan breathed. "This might have been a bad idea."

The tombstone continued to push out of the ground, reaching the height of a small tree. It still clicked away madly, and new bits swung open. Enough of the interior of the tombstone had been pulled apart that one could see a small chamber inside.

There was something inside the chamber.

Something moving.

It was too dark to see it properly, but the thing inside was rising and falling, like it was filling with air.

Jonathan reached for his flashlight, but Jake grabbed hold of him.

"Don't," Jake warned, keeping his voice low.

Jonathan nodded quickly. Jake could see fear in his friend's eyes. "What do we do?"

Jake turned back to the tombstone. The ground had stopped rumbling. The stone was now pushed as far out of the ground as it would go. It had stopped clicking. All the parts of it that could flip open had done so.

A jet of steam issued forth from the inner chamber. Jake's eyes tried to spy what lay behind the cloud of white-hot vapour. He couldn't make out any true shape or form.

The thing inside gave several rasping, grating breaths. One fact remained: whatever was inside of the stone was alive.

Jake got to his feet. His knees threatened to buckle from under him. His heart pounded in his chest. He took a step closer to the tombstone, if you could call it a tombstone.

The thing seemed to sense Jake's approach. Its breathing quickened.

Jake strained to see through the billowing steam.

Somewhere in that tombstone was the core. If he could take it out, maybe the doors would swing shut, trapping whatever was in there back inside the chamber. He'd worry about his hand and eye later.

Jake took a step forward.

"Jake ..."

Behind him, Jonathan grabbed the flashlight and aimed the beam dead ahead through the steam.

For just a moment, Jake saw the thing.

A living skeleton — not remotely human — let out a shriek, threw open its jaws, and lashed out —

Jonathan screamed. He dropped the flashlight.

The thing clamped its arms onto Jake's shoulders. The force of the blow threw him to his knees. He opened his mouth to cry out, but the thing squeezed, taking the wind from Jake's lungs.

Behind him, Jonathan found the flashlight again and pointed the beam at the creature.

It was a black, dripping thing, like a skeleton smeared with an oil slick. Although the skeleton stood on two legs, it wasn't human. The vertebrae on the back were hunched and curved, continuing long past the back to form a tail. The creature's face kept changing shape, like it was trying several different ones at once. The only things that remained the same were the sharp black teeth and its penetrating stare.

The eyes remained locked on Jake as the creature continued to change.

The tail melted away.

The black, oily film pulled tight against the creature's body. It changed in colour to match human skin. Jake's skin, to be exact.

Hair grew from the monster's head. Jake's hair.

And clothes. The creature was even growing clothes over its body.

Jake's clothes.

Jonathan watched in horror as the thing pinning Jake to the ground finished transforming itself into ... well ... *Jake*.

"What are you doing to me?" Jake shouted.

"What are you doing to me?" the creature shouted back, its voice deep and guttural.

"Stop it! Let me go!"

"Stop it! Let me go!" the creature repeated, this time modulating its voice to a higher pitch. The voice was too high this time, almost like the thing had downed a tank of helium. "Stop it! Let me go! Stop it! Let me go!" it kept repeating, until the voice matched Jake's.

The thing holding Jake down smiled.

Without releasing its grip, it lifted Jake off the ground and stretched its arms into the air, so that Jake's legs dangled helplessly. Whatever it was, the thing was stronger than Jake. Stronger than both of them put together.

The thing turned around and tossed Jake into the chamber, like an old apple core. Jake thumped against the stone wall and let out a whimper of pain.

Then the creature bent down and yanked something out of the tombstone.

The core.

At once, the clicking could be heard again. Pieces of

stone started to swing back, hundreds of little iron scraps being drawn into one giant lodestone. Jake tried to step out of the chamber, but his feet were already bolted in. His hands, at his sides, were also fixed in place.

The stones kept snapping back into place. Jake felt the stone begin to take on a new state, forming a thick liquid around his arms and legs. It was filling in the gaps, trapping Jake in the stone itself.

The stones flipped back around part of his head, covering his nose. Jake gasped, getting a whiff of a metallic scent. Then the stone reshaped, oozing around his nostrils. How was he going to breathe?!

"Jonathan!" he screamed, feeling the stones lock around the lower portion of his face.

Jonathan, still pointing the flashlight in Jake's direction, stood mute with horror.

"Jonath—"

A stone clicked into place over Jake's mouth.

The thing that looked like Jake took a few steps toward Jonathan. Instinctively, Jonathan backed away. "No," he muttered. "Don't come any closer."

The creature loomed into view, a twisted parody of Jake. He smiled from ear to ear. The creature stretched the smile wider than any human smile should have gone. Although the monster had turned most of its teeth human, there was still a row at the back that was inky black, and sharp as nails.

Jonathan looked over the creature's shoulder to see the last piece of the tombstone snap shut, locking Jake away.

"No!"

The tombstone began to lower itself into the ground. Not all the way. There was still a small mound left over when it had settled. Enough to make the stone resemble what Jake and Jonathan had thought was merely a tombstone.

Jonathan stood with his back against a tree, staring into the eyes of the thing that had taken over Jake's body.

The creature looked at Jonathan. "Hello, friend," it said. It was Jake's voice, all right, but it wasn't friendly.

"What are you?"

"I'm Jake," the creature smiled.

Jonathan shook his head. "Give me the core!"

The creature just grinned its impossible grin. It shook its head. "But I'm free now."

"What about Jake?"

"I told you, I *am* Jake. At least, I'm Jake now. I've been so many things over the years. I can be Jake for a long, long time."

"What about me?"

"What about you?"

"I've seen everything. I can tell others what you are."

"Who is going to believe you? Especially without the core."

The creature seemed to have this all figured out. "What do you want?"

The thing didn't respond. It pocketed the core, turned away, and walked off into the night.

Jonathan stood against the tree for a long time. He kept his eyes fixed on the tombstone.

When he felt the thing had been gone long enough for it to be safe, Jonathan stepped away from the tree and hobbled over to the tombstone. His body quaked with fear and exhaustion.

Jonathan dropped to his knees and pressed his palms

against the stone.

"Jake?" he called out. "Are you there?"

The tombstone felt cold against his hands. He could no longer see any cracks or splits in the stone. It was smooth and polished. It would be impossible to get inside without that core.

Was Jake even alive in there?

Jonathan's eyes stung. Hot, salty tears dripped down his face. Why couldn't he have done more? Why didn't he stand up against that creature?

He'd been a fan of scary things his whole life. Why chicken out now?

Jonathan slunk away into the night.

Chicken. That's what he was. Just a dumb, feather-brained, scaredy-cat chicken.

What was he going to do now?

It was more than late by the time Jonathan got back home. He didn't feel like talking to his parents. He didn't feel like much of anything. He just went upstairs to his room, shut the door, and lay down on his bed.

For a little while, his body shook with sobs.

Then Jonathan lay there and stared at the ceiling. He was exhausted, but he couldn't sleep. His mind kept replaying the events of the evening over and over again. Images of the creature kept flashing in his head. And of Jake, his final scream, and the tombstone sealing him in.

Tomorrow, he was going to have to show up at school. And that thing was going to be there.

CHAPTER 11

"Are you all right?" Jonathan's mother asked the next morning. She'd been watching Jonathan dig his spoon into his bowl of Corn Flakes over and over again without taking a bite.

What could Jonathan say? That he'd stayed up all night sobbing to himself? That he hadn't slept at all, and probably wouldn't ever again? That his best friend in the world was trapped in a hunk of stone and buried in the ground with it? That the person who appeared to be his best friend was some shape-shifting monster? His parents would just tell him to stop watching so many scary movies.

"I'm fine," Jonathan said, jamming his first spoonful of cereal into his mouth. He sat there crunching it into a pasty ball, forgetting to swallow. He'd lost his voracious appetite. He could barely even look at food right now.

"You're sure you're okay?" Jonathan's mother tried again.

Jonathan nodded glumly.

The phone rang.

Jonathan's mother picked it up. She exchanged a few

words with whoever was on the other line and then handed the receiver to her son. "It's for you."

Jonathan wrinkled his brow. He picked up the phone and held it to his ear. "Hello?"

"Good morning, friend."

His heart seemed to stop, or burst, or stop and burst. It took a second to realize that it had done neither. When he was satisfied that his heart was still beating, Jonathan let out a long, shaky breath. "What do you want?"

"I wanted to make sure you were feeling all right," the creature replied. It was using Jake's voice so perfectly that Jonathan felt sick to his stomach to hear it. "You were quite upset last night."

"Stop it," Jonathan snapped. So what if his mother saw him acting upset on the phone? This monster was just tormenting him now.

"I'm sorry," the creature returned. "I wanted to ask you about school. I'm still learning the ropes, and I hear I've got an in-school suspension today. Maybe you could help show me around."

"I don't think so," Jonathan returned.

"Right now, you're the only friend Jake has," the creature said. "But I could make more friends." There was something about the way the creature said it that made Jonathan uneasy. What business did it have making friends? What did it need other people for?

"I'll see you when the bell rings," Jonathan muttered. "We line up outside the junior doors."

"The junior doors," the creature returned. "At what time?"

"Eight-forty-five."

"I do so look forward to seeing you," the creature said. "Have a pleasant breakfast."

And with that, the phone line went dead.

Jonathan was still cradling the receiver to his ear when his mother approached and took it from him. "What did Jake want?"

"Uh, nothing much. Just to see how I was doing."

"That Jake," she smiled, "is such a nice boy. He really is the best friend you've ever had."

Other Jake, as Jonathan was now referring to the creature impersonating his best friend, did not know where Jonathan and Real Jake hung out before school. That was good. Jonathan didn't want to see him any more than he had to.

He snuck around to the back of the school. Jonathan hadn't quite reached the other side of the building when a figure came walking around to greet him.

Jonathan stopped in his tracks. It was Other Jake.

"*There* you are," the thing impersonating Jake said.

Jonathan shifted his gaze to the one door Mr. Roberts, the caretaker, used. It was shut. So it was just the two of them behind the school. Other Jake could do whatever he wanted to Jonathan here. Nobody would be the wiser. At least, not until the caretaker came out to mow the grass, but he'd just recently cut it. If Other Jake snuffed the life out of Jonathan, it might be days before anyone found him here.

"I thought you wanted to meet at the junior doors," Other Jake continued. "What are you doing here?" There was nothing threatening about the way Other Jake spoke, except that Other Jake only spoke pleasantly. It was as if the creature behind the disguise hadn't learned enough about humans to make a truly convincing impersonation. This was its best effort at being human.

Jonathan said nothing.

"Did you come here to hide from me?"

Of course he had. Jonathan could barely stand to look this hideous impersonation of his best friend in the eyes, but he dared not admit it.

Other Jake just stared at him.

Other Jake didn't blink his eyes as often as a normal person did. When he did blink, it seemed forced. It was as if Other Jake had to remind himself that normal people blinked. "I was looking for you," he said after a moment.

"Why?"

"Because we're friends, you and I. And I need you to go on being my friend."

"Jake is my friend. Not you."

Other Jake shook his head. "When are you going to realize that I am Jake now? I look like him. I sound like him. And I'm learning a lot about him. Soon, nobody will be able to tell the difference. Not even you," Other Jake said, in a tone that set Jonathan's hairs on end.

"I'd know."

Other Jake shrugged. "Trust me, it's easier if you go along with it."

Jonathan tried to swallow the lump in his throat. "You … you make it seem like you've done this sort of thing before."

Other Jake nodded very slowly, and very deliberately.

"What happens when you're finished being Jake?"

Other Jake gave a sideways look and shrugged. "Oh, there's always somebody new I can be."

What was this thing? It looked like a boy, but Jonathan had the feeling it was much older. It was the kind of thing that might have been around, like, forever.

"Why don't we go back and spend time with the other children?"

"Good idea." Jonathan nodded. Anything to get him and the creature out in the open.

As he moved past Other Jake to head to the schoolyard, he heard Other Jake remark from behind, "Thanks for showing me this spot. It looks like a good place to have a snack."

Other Jake had peeled his lips back far enough for Jonathan to get a look at the needle-like teeth beyond the molars.

The school bell rang.

"Looks like I have to go and serve detention," Other Jake chirped. "See you around."

The rest of the school day was agony. Sure, Other Jake wasn't in the room with him, but all Jonathan could do was obsess about his best friend buried in the ground, and the new impostor taking his place.

As soon as school ended, Jonathan raced to get out of the building before Other Jake could follow him. He looked over his shoulder. Already he could spy Other Jake heading his way, a smile on his face.

Jonathan darted towards the bike rack. He found his bike, then dropped to his knees and fumbled with the combination lock. *Please*, he thought to himself, *let me unlock this before Other Jake gets here.*

"Jonathan!" Other Jake called out.

Jonathan said nothing. He sped away on the bicycle, nearly plowing over a small group of Grade 3s on his way out, and almost collided with an oncoming car. Jonathan screeched the bike to a halt as the car horn blared at him from the street. He stood at the edge of the road, panting heavily, and turned back. Way at the other end of the schoolyard was Other Jake. He was staring past the throngs of other kids at school, eyes glued on Jonathan.

Jonathan let out a shaky breath, got back onto his bike, and pedalled down the street. He didn't stop pedalling for a long time. Long enough to leave the school far behind him, and Other Jake, who did not have a bike, in the dust.

Jonathan squeezed the brakes and dropped his feet to the pavement. He looked slowly over his shoulder and scanned the surroundings. A few cars whizzed past him on the street. The odd pedestrian sauntered by without giving him a second look. The town, as far as Jonathan knew it, was peaceful.

There was no one he could share any of this with.

The tears came on suddenly. They stung his eyes and spilled down his cheeks. He let out a few sobs, and that caused the rest to come flooding out.

He must have looked like an idiot standing there on the sidewalk, crying for no apparent reason. He let it all out. Jonathan wasn't sure how long he cried for. It felt like half an hour.

When he was through, Jonathan wiped his nose on his sleeve and took a deep breath.

He would not cry anymore. He was strong, and he would not let this horror get the better of him.

Besides, now Jonathan knew where he had to go.

Jonathan didn't stop pedalling until he reached the one place he might be able to get some answers. He walked his bike up along with him, to the front of the house, and then banged on the door. Hard.

He looked over his shoulder. There was no sign of Other Jake, just a few pedestrians walking by and the occasional car zipping along the street.

The door opened a crack. A familiar face peered out through the narrow strip of darkness. Crumb.

"You!" Crumb blurted, his look of curiosity soon switching to annoyance and anger. He looked around beyond Jonathan. "Where's your friend?"

"It's kind of hard to explain."

But Crumb had already moved on to the next piece of business. "Where's the core?"

"Uh … it's kind of … gone."

"What do you mean, *gone*?"

Jonathan looked over his shoulder yet again. It was possible that Other Jake might have followed him here. The creature masquerading as Jake had the ability to transform itself. What made Jonathan think it couldn't switch forms into one of the pedestrians walking down the street? Or even Crumb?

Jonathan shook the idea from his mind. Crumb was Crumb. He wouldn't be asking about the core if he were somebody else.

"Can I come inside?"

Crumb narrowed his eyes. "After what you did last time?"

"Please. It's about the core. And my friend Jake."

Crumb looked long and hard at Jonathan, then stepped aside and let him in.

Jonathan explained everything. The core. The tombstone. The creature locked within, and where Jake was now, well, *buried*. He hadn't been able to tell anyone about this. Certainly not his parents. They would have never believed him. Jonathan only managed to get the essentials of the story out and broke down into a sobbing fit.

"He's dead. Jake's dead, and it's all my fault!"

"What makes you think he's dead?"

Jonathan couldn't believe what he was hearing. "He got locked up in a stone. The stone went under the ground. How can you imagine anyone surviving that?"

Crumb nodded. "You've got a point. But this other creature seems to have done just fine."

"Yeah. You know how I might be able to stop it?"

"What makes you think I would know something about that?"

"You had the core once."

"I never put it into the tombstone," Crumb grumbled. "And I did warn you."

A long silence passed between them.

Eventually, Crumb looked away. "Do you not have anything which might give us some clues?"

"Well," Jonathan shrugged, "we can always go check out that tombstone again."

Crumb waved him off. "Look at me. I can barely open the fridge. You think I'm in any position to go down that steep hill in my condition?"

Jonathan shook his head. A thought struck him. He dug into his pocket and pulled out his smart phone. "I did get a ton of shots of the area. Here, check it out."

He started scrolling through his saved photo albums. Most of them involved all sorts of gory makeup effects that

Jonathan had been trying out for fun, or weird and crazy self-portraits that Jonathan had souped up on his computer. Soon he found the folder with all of the class trip pictures, and handed the phone to Crumb.

"What am I supposed to do with this thing?"

Jonathan wrinkled his brow. "You know, you scroll through it. With your finger." Jonathan showed Crumb what to do.

Crumb shook his head. "I think I preferred digital watches," he grumbled, and scanned through the pictures.

Crumb stopped suddenly. His eyes widened.

"Find something?" Jonathan asked.

"That's impossible," Crumb gasped, his voice a whisper.

"What? A class trip to the cemetery? I thought so too, but there you have it."

"No, not that." Crumb held the phone closer to his face so he could get a real good look at the image. "It's uncanny."

"What is?"

Crumb turned the phone and pointed the image to Jonathan. It was a picture of Jonathan pulling his cheeks apart and sticking his tongue out. Behind him, Mr. Glick looked on, annoyed.

"But that's not a photo of the cemetery. That's just us goofing around on the bus."

Crumb shook his head. "Look at that man behind you. Your teacher, Mr. Glick —"

"— has no style whatsoever. I know," Jonathan interrupted.

"No. Shut up, little fool, and let me talk."

Jonathan stared at the old man. His words were harsh,

but there was fear in his eyes.

"That man — your teacher …" Shawn Crumb gulped. "He was my teacher, too."

Jonathan just looked at him. "And you're calling me the fool?"

Crumb grumbled. "I'm not making this up. I can't explain it. He doesn't look like he's aged a day."

"No, you've got it wrong," Jonathan replied, snatching the phone back. "Mr. Glick said his grandfather was also a teacher. There must be some kind of family resemblance, that's all."

Crumb shook his head. "I never forget a face. It's no resemblance. It's the same man! This Mr. Glick is the one who gave our class the local history assignment in the first place. Without that project I never would have come across the cemetery."

"But that's impossible," Jonathan spat. "There's no way Glick could have been the same age back then as he is now."

Crumb shrugged. "There's a connection," he mused. "You need to find it."

"Why me?"

"It's not my problem anymore," Crumb said sourly.

"Unless I go and tell Glick that I know *who* you are and *where* you are," Jonathan returned, his frustration welling.

Crumb fixed Jonathan with a long, mean stare. "Fine," he said after a moment's consideration. "But you still need to do the dirty work on your own. I can barely even hobble to the bathroom, let alone take on Mr. Glick."

Jonathan let out a long sigh. "It's not as if I can ask him directly. Then he'd know."

"You'll have to search through his stuff. Maybe find a

clue." Crumb's eyes brightened. "Glick was the one who brought us to the cemetery in the first place, wasn't he?"

"Yeah, so?"

"Maybe he did it for a reason. Maybe he was looking for something. Or maybe he wanted us to find something. Maybe we did exactly what he wanted us to: find that tombstone. Get the core. And open it."

Jonathan shook his head. "You think he's in on the whole thing?"

"Give me those pictures you took again."

Jonathan begrudgingly handed the phone back to Crumb. The old man leaned in close, trying to get a good look at the photographs on the display.

Crumb's eyes widened as the magnification increased. "There it is. Don't you see it?"

Jonathan looked over Crumb's shoulder. "What, Mr. Glick's shirt pocket? Because that's what you've zoomed into."

"Not the pocket," Crumb replied, jabbing a finger at the image on the screen. "Look what he's got inside it."

Jonathan had to narrow his eyes to bring the image into focus. "Oh," he said at last.

Poking out of Glick's pocket was a small, dark object. It was the size and shape of a sleek smart phone, only it wasn't a phone. The object was jet black and shaped like the tombstone Jake was now trapped in, even down to the two spike-like protrusions on either side of the top. To Jonathan, they resembled the horns of a dangerous animal.

"What is that thing?"

Crumb turned to Jonathan. "Tell me you have some pictures of that tombstone."

"I have some pictures of that tombstone," Jonathan repeated.

"Show me!"

Jonathan started to shuffle through the pictures of the tombstone he'd taken. Crumb nodded as the images whizzed by, then he extended a shaky finger and told Jonathan to stop and magnify the image.

Jonathan did so. They were looking at the rear of the tombstone. It was a good thing Jonathan had used a high resolution, because even at ten megapixels, the image was starting to lose focus. Still, Jonathan could see what had Crumb so excited.

There were two small indentations in the back of the tombstone. They were too perfect to have been caused by wear and tear. The two slits were the perfect size and shape for the spiky ends of the thing in Glick's breast pocket.

"Mr. Glick's got another core," Jonathan breathed.

Crumb nodded. "Find that, and you might have something to bargain with."

For the first time since they had met, Jonathan got the feeling that Shawn Crumb might be on to something.

Pedalling his bike home, Jonathan wasn't sure what role Mr. Glick had to play in all of this. There was no way a person could go on looking the same for so many years. Some people looked the spitting image of their parents or grandparents. Maybe that's what happened with the kids of the Glick family. It made more sense than what Crumb had to say.

Then again, there was little logic in this whole Other Jake business. If there was logic in any of this, a real explanation that Jonathan could understand, he didn't get it. Still, there wasn't time to worry about Glick. Other Jake would be after him, and as for Mr. Glick — well, Jonathan would deal with him when he needed to.

The real problem was that there was no one Jonathan could turn to now. Crumb was too old to help him in any real way, other than act all crabby and drop weird clues like he just had.

He was alone in this now.

The red glow of a stoplight caught Jonathan's attention. He squeezed the brakes, bringing the bike to a halt.

Standing in one of the main intersections, Jonathan cast a glance at the flow of traffic moving across the road. It wasn't a big town by any means, but big enough. On this street alone, there were three doughnut shops, a video store, the old bookstore, a submarine sandwich place, that big grocery store, and —

Jonathan clutched the handlebars of the bike.

Other Jake!

He was standing at one of the side doors to the big grocery store. The door was propped open so that Jonathan could clearly see one of the cashiers holding something. She was a big, meaty woman with thick curly hair and floppy cheeks. In her hands, she held a big brown paper bag that overflowed with bits and pieces of old cash registers.

Above, the light turned green.

Jonathan stood frozen in fear, but also in fascination. What was going on?

The woman was giving the bag to Other Jake. It was just junk, right? Old bits of circuit boards, digital readout panels, and wiring, stuffed into a bag.

The person in the car behind Jonathan honked the horn loudly.

Other Jake and the cashier looked up. Their eyes met Jonathan's. For a moment, Jonathan wondered if they might scream, or even duck into the building to avoid being noticed. But no. What they did just chilled Jonathan even further. They both just looked at him and smiled.

"Move your bike, kid!" an angry voice jabbed from behind.

Jonathan turned his head back to see some eighty-year-old grandpa with the car window down, shaking his fist at him.

Jonathan blinked, righted himself on the bike, and pedalled through the intersection.

As he glanced back at the doorway, Jonathan could no longer see Other Jake or the grocery store cashier.

Looking over his shoulder, Jonathan only saw cars and angry drivers.

He raced home, wondering whether or not he was being followed.

As soon as he returned home, Jonathan went up to his room. He still had no idea how to stop Other Jake besides stealing back the core and trying to stick it in the tombstone.

There was a knock at the door.

"Not now," he moaned.

There was another knock. Jonathan straightened himself up. Another knock. He went over to the door, and stopped. The knocking wasn't coming from the door.

It was coming from the window.

Jonathan paced to the window, reached out for the blind,

and opened it. Then he jammed his fist into his opened mouth to keep from screaming.

A floating eye hovered outside the window.

Jake's eye.

Jonathan stared in unblinking amazement at it. He must've been staring at it for longer than the eye had hoped. It bonked angrily against the side of the window. Jonathan quickly opened it, and the eye floated into the room.

"Jake? Is that you?!"

The eye hovered in the air, regarding him. What kind of question was this? Who else had a floating eye?

"I was so worried. I thought I'd never see you again —" Jonathan stopped himself, thinking this through. "I mean, you're still trapped in that tombstone, right?"

The eye just stared at him, levitating over Jonathan's shelf full of horror movie action figures.

"Hang on, you're just an eye now! You can't hear what I'm saying."

The eye said nothing. It was, after all, just an eye.

"You can't read my lips. You can just stare."

Jonathan moved away from the window and over to his desktop computer. He fired it up and opened his word processing program. He was aware of the eye hovering over his shoulder. The hairs at the back of his neck prickled. It was one thing when Jake was in the room with the disembodied eye, but Jake was buried under the ground. Was it possible that Jake wasn't even alive anymore, that this floating eye was all that was left of him? If so, did the eye even have a brain to control it?

Jonathan shook the ideas out of his mind. He didn't want to think about Jake being gone. If the eye was here, that meant Jake was still alive.

Wait.

What if the eye belonged to that *thing*?

What if the eye was only here to spy on Jonathan?

He didn't know much about the creature. But if it could change its form to make itself look like Jake, then what couldn't it do?

Jonathan drummed his fingers against the bottom of the keyboard, thinking things through. Then he typed:

IF YOU REALLY ARE JAKE'S EYE, THEN WHAT HAPPENED TO YOU LAST SUMMER DURING BASEBALL?

a) You choked on your own saliva

b) You tripped over first base

c) You puked on the first base coach

d) All of the above

Jonathan looked over his shoulder at the eye. He could tell it was scanning the words, but who was reading them?

Then Jonathan turned back to the computer and typed: JUST MOVE OVER TO THE RIGHT ANSWER.

Feeling uneasy about being too close to the eye, Jonathan pushed his chair aside. Once he was out of the way, the eye loomed into view. This still gave an evil eye a one-in-four chance of bluffing a correct answer, but at least it was something.

The eye moved over to option c).

Jonathan smiled.

He slid his chair back to the computer, caring less that he was literally eye to eye with the eye. He typed: I'M GOING

TO TYPE OUT "YES" AND "NO" ON THE SCREEN. AFTER I FINISH TYPING, YOU JUST FLOAT OVER TO THE RIGHT ANSWER.

Jonathan typed in the answer keys, then continued: ARE YOU HURT?

No, the eye replied.

ARE YOU TRAPPED?

Yes.

IN THE TOMBSTONE? Jonathan added.

Yes.

Jonathan looked at the eye. He tried to imagine what Jake was going through in the tombstone. He really couldn't call it a tombstone anymore. It was more like some sort of prison for that monster.

Jake was buried alive in there. Frantically, Jonathan typed: DO YOU HAVE ENOUGH AIR?

The eye didn't respond at first. Then it moved over to the *Yes*. Maybe Jake didn't need air while he was trapped in the tombstone. Maybe it sort of put you in suspended animation. He hoped that was the case — if not, where would Jake get the air he needed? How would he go to the bathroom? Eat or drink?

Jonathan remembered that Jake hated being shut into tight spaces. Claustrophobia. That's what it was called. Jake had a pretty bad case of it — ever since that soccer game in third grade when the other team piled up on him.

Jonathan looked at the eye, then typed: CAN YOU FEEL THE TOMBSTONE AROUND YOU?

Yes, the eye responded.

The way the eye flew over to the *Yes* response, Jonathan could have sworn that Jake was screaming out the answer. He imagined himself in Jake's position — trapped on all sides, deep under the ground, with no way out — no way to communicate, except that eye. It was one thing to be smothered and have no idea what was happening around you. But the eye could show Jake what the world was like, and somehow that made it worse.

Cripes. How was Jonathan going to do this? He obviously needed to get the core back. Not to mention the other core from Mr. Glick. But getting either core wasn't going to be easy. He'd seen the jaws and teeth on that thing in its true form. What would it do to protect itself? And what tricks did Mr. Glick have up his sleeve?

Jonathan loved scary things when they were imaginary. Now he was going to have to confront a *real-life* scary thing. A real-life scary thing with teeth. A real-life scary thing that could kill him.

Jonathan turned to the eye — all that was left of his best friend — and let out a deep sigh. Then he typed: ARE YOU SCARED?

The eye floated over to respond *Yes.*

Jonathan nodded.

SO AM I, he typed.

CHAPTER 12

It was essential that Jonathan get to school early.

To do so, he needed a convincing story. The best Jonathan could think of was that Mr. Glick had asked him to swing by before the bell rang for some extra help in math.

It was the first time Jonathan's parents had ever seen or heard him take any interest in staying on top of his schoolwork. They did not ask why he needed to be at school an hour before it opened.

This was all part of the plan.

Jonathan tried to remain calm and quiet on the car ride to school, even though his heart was beating a mile a minute. What if the plan didn't work? What if he got caught?

There was no time for any what-ifs.

His mother pulled the car into the front parking lot to find the school completely devoid of life. The school was as still as a painting, except for the breeze blowing the nearby tree branches.

Jonathan's mother turned to face him in the back seat. "You're sure Mr. Glick said for you to meet him here?"

Jonathan nodded emphatically. "Oh, yes! Seven-thirty.

That's what he said."

Jonathan's mother looked from her son to the empty parking lot, and back to her son once more. Several thoughts shuffled through her mind, which was already clogged with things that needed to get done at her job.

"Don't work too hard," she mused, and leaned over to kiss Jonathan on the forehead. Jonathan squirmed at the sight of his mother's lips. Thank goodness nobody was around to see it.

After escaping his mother's kiss, and making sure that the car was safely out of the lot, Jonathan began to tiptoe around the school. He edged to the far side of the building where he and Jake liked to hang out together.

Although no teachers were at school yet, Jonathan didn't want to risk it. He crouched low and ducked past the classrooms on the ground floor, all the while keeping his eye on the prize.

Jonathan had hung out at the back of the school long enough to learn that if he wanted to sneak inside, all he had to do was wait for the caretaker to come by and open the rear door. Mr. Roberts always kept it propped open in case he wanted to come out for a cigarette, or fresh air, or whatever.

Jonathan eyed the door.

He dug his fingers into the tiny slit between the door and the frame and pulled.

"Yes!"

Jonathan pulled the door open and peered into the boiler room. Several large pieces of machinery chugged away, filling the place with metallic echoes. Jonathan shuffled inside, casting glances every which way. It was imperative that the grizzly caretaker did not see him.

Edging inside, Jonathan caught a glimpse of a human-shaped shadow cast along the wall.

Mr. Roberts sat in his office, bopping his head to the classic rock radio tunes filling the room.

Jonathan caught sight of his reflection in the far mirror and froze. His image was in plain view of Mr. Roberts, including that look of panic on his face. Jonathan held the pose for at least ten seconds before it occurred to him that Mr. Roberts hadn't seen him. In a flash, Jonathan ducked down, shuffled past Mr. Roberts, went out another door, and darted into the school hallway. Very quietly, he closed the door behind him and let out the breath he'd been holding onto for the last minute or so. It came out of him in one long, shaky spasm. He'd made it inside. Now came the hard part.

Jonathan had never seen the school like this. For one thing, the halls were completely empty. Sure, a few stray schoolbags and shoes lay scattered along the edges by the coat hooks, but the school was otherwise vacant.

It was dark, too. Jonathan hadn't realized what a good a job those fluorescent lights did lighting the place up. Despite all of the classroom windows, very little of the outside light penetrated the long, empty hallway.

Jonathan edged forward. Although Mr. Roberts was busy rocking out to the radio, who knew when he'd start pacing about the school making sure everything was in order?

There wasn't much time.

Jonathan glanced at a clock hanging at the top of the doorway to find it was already a quarter to eight. In the distance, he heard the rumble of a car's engine.

Teachers were starting to arrive.

He had to be quick.

Backpack slung over his shoulder, Jonathan made his way down the hallway, rounded a corner, and stopped just outside of Mr. Glick's room.

He put his hand on the doorknob and gave it a turn. The door creaked open. Jonathan let out a sigh of relief. Mr. Roberts hadn't cleaned up the classroom yet, which meant that the door was still unlocked.

As he entered the room, Jonathan made sure to pull the shade covering the window down so that no one could look in and spy on him. Then he shuffled over to Mr. Glick's desk and curled his fingers around the handle to the desk drawer.

Many students had tried to get into Mr. Glick's desk drawer over the course of the year, because Mr. Glick had a habit of confiscating toys and various fun things that his students liked to play with: toy cars, monster cards, rude erasers, you name it. Glick enjoyed watching the expressions on his students' faces as he took their prized possessions and casually tossed them away into that drawer of his, never to be seen again.

Nobody could get into that drawer, and Jonathan realized that it was probably the perfect place to slip some sort of monstrous core he might take along on a field trip.

Jonathan pulled on the drawer. It moved about half an inch, and then stopped from the force of the lock holding it in place.

He had expected as much.

Jonathan dug into his pocket, pulled out a small jar, and carefully unscrewed the lid.

Jake's eye slowly levitated out of the jar and hovered in the air momentarily. It exchanged a wordless glance with Jonathan, who pointed to the small gap in Glick's desk drawer. It

126

was too small for Jonathan to wedge his hand in, but just big enough for the eye to squeeze through.

All Jonathan had to do was shine a little light in there from the penlight he'd smuggled into the room, and see what the eye turned up. If the other core happened to be there, then Jonathan would find a way to break it out.

He held the drawer partly open with one hand, and focused the penlight beam into the crack with the other. His heart was pounding so heavily that he didn't hear the footsteps until they were getting too loud for comfort.

Jonathan opened his mouth to warn the eye. But Jake's eye couldn't hear. It wouldn't be able to even feel Jake jostle the desk drawer — and he couldn't jostle it now. Whoever was at the door would hear him.

Jonathan ducked under the desk, hoping that the footsteps would fade away.

Instead they came to a stop outside the door. Jonathan heard the doorknob twist, and the sound of someone trying the door.

Under the desk, Jonathan clenched his teeth. Next came the jiggle of keys in the lock.

Cripes!

Jonathan bolted up from under the desk and strode over to the window. He fumbled with the latches and managed to push the window open.

Behind him, the door began to creak open.

There was no time to worry about the mesh screen blocking his path now. Jonathan pushed the screen so hard it popped out of the window and he leapt out. He and his backpack came tumbling down to the dewy grass with barely a sound.

Then he was on his feet and running, his mind racing with panic, and one thought that wouldn't leave: Jake's eye was still there, locked in Mr. Glick's desk.

The next hour or so felt like days. Jonathan had escaped into the schoolyard, ducked behind a tree, and waited for other kids to trickle onto the playground. He only emerged when a sizable crowd formed so he could fit in unnoticed. Did it matter, though? If Glick had seen, or even suspected Jonathan, he didn't need to come barging onto the playground to nab him.

Jonathan kept looking over his shoulder as the minutes ticked by like eons. There was Other Jake, smiling at Jonathan in the distance, walking the perimeter of the playground over and over again. All the while, he kept glancing at Jonathan, smiling and waving.

Eventually, the bell rang and the students lined up. Jonathan shuffled inside, hung up his coat, got his books, and tried to avoid looking at Mr. Glick as he sat down at his desk.

All he could think about was not getting caught, and how in the world he was going to rescue Jake's eye.

Jonathan sat rigid in his seat as Mr. Glick took morning attendance.

The list of threatening people in the classroom was quickly expanding. First Darryl Richter and his arsenal of idiots, then Other Jake, and now Mr. Glick himself. Mr. Glick hadn't seemed mysterious all year. If anything, he got annoyed by Jonathan's antics pretty easily. Jonathan had served more than his fair share of detentions over the course of the year.

Still, after last night's encounter with Shawn Crumb,

Jonathan could not take his eyes off Mr. Glick. Was it worth approaching him about what had happened to Jake? Or was Mr. Glick somehow in on this too?

He felt a prickle along his spine — the kind of goose-bumpy feeling he got from staying up late to watch horror movies on TV. There was a taste of iron on his tongue, as if he'd swallowed blood. Jonathan turned and looked over his shoulder.

Other Jake was smiling at him.

What was with that creepy smile? Was he purposely trying to freak Jonathan out? Or was it Other Jake's impression of being a human, trying to fit in by smiling?

Jonathan found it in himself to smile back. Other Jake clearly had his secrets, but so did Jonathan.

As Mr. Glick got the class started on some silly reading assignment, Jonathan turned his head to stare out the window. He was fortunate to have a seat beside the window this term, although he generally preferred to be closest to the bank of computers, which meant he could slide over there and play video games after rushing through his work. But the window had merit, too. If you didn't want to stare at Mr. Glick or the notes he scribbled on the chalkboard, the window gave a view of the side of the school with the grassy hill, and Jake's eye, and —

The eye!

It had escaped somehow. Now it lay in the windowsill, staring at Jonathan.

Jonathan scribbled something on a paper and held it up to the eye.

GET OUT. HE CAN SEE YOU.

Jonathan could see the pupil of the eye dilate in an attempt to read his writing. What was Jake up to? Anyone in Jonathan's row might turn to see the eye floating there, and then what?

How could the eye escape without being seen? It would have to wait there until everybody cleared out of the room, including Mr. Glick!

Hang on a second. The eye wasn't looking at him anymore. It was scanning along past Jonathan, along the rows of students. Jonathan followed the eye's trajectory, and found himself looking at Other Jake.

For once, Other Jake wasn't staring back at Jonathan.

He was staring at the eye.

Other Jake's expression changed. His own eyes flashed into two pinpoints of fury. The whites of his eyes rolled over. For a split second, Other Jake glared with two black, inhuman orbs. The creature clenched his fists, and his pupils contracted, not to dots, but to two vertical slits.

Other Jake blinked, and his eyes changed back to resemble Real Jake's eyes.

Jonathan scribbled something down on the paper and held it up to the window, but the eye was gone.

Once again, he felt that prickling sensation along his back and skin. It was stronger now, causing an itchy feeling that was hard to ignore. The iron taste in his mouth was so strong that he nearly gagged then and there.

Jonathan turned to find Other Jake staring at him again. This time, there was no smile on his face. An observer might suggest that Other Jake didn't have any expression, but the observer would be wrong. There was something cold and calculating about this look that was even more chilling than the smile. Other Jake now knew that the eye had escaped, and that Jonathan was conspiring to help his friend.

Ever since last night, Other Jake had been playing a game with Jonathan: go on being his best friend or else. Now there was no hiding the fact that Jonathan was not going to play the best friend. There was just the or else.

"*'Get out. He can see you'*?" a voice called out from above him.

Jonathan looked up. Mr. Glick was reading the last note he'd scribbled on the paper. Why was it that teachers always felt the need to read private notes aloud? "What are you writing about, Jonathan?"

There were a few mixed giggles in the class, most of them coming from Darryl Richter and his friends.

Jonathan swallowed hard. It felt like someone had jammed a rock down his throat. Other Jake was now smiling, and waving to Mr. Glick. "I can see you too!"

More laughter.

Jonathan's face reddened.

"What I don't see is your homework," Mr. Glick stated.

"Oh."

Jonathan rummaged through his desk for his math textbook and notebook. His desk was never the most organized; shift one book the wrong way, and they would all fall out.

Jonathan attempted to fish out his homework.

The books all fell out.

More laughter.

Jonathan fumed and bent down to pick them up.

"Can I put an answer on the board?" Other Jake called out.

Jonathan narrowed his eyes. Other Jake must not have known that Jake was terrible at math.

131

It even threw Mr. Glick for a loop. "Are you sure?"

"Sure I'm sure. I've got them all done. See?"

Jonathan peered over the edge of his desk to see Other Jake holding up a math notebook.

Mr. Glick shrugged. "Have fun."

From his vantage point down near the ground, Jonathan watched Other Jake march up to the front of the blackboard. He plucked a piece of chalk out of a box on the ledge and immediately began to scribble out the answer.

What was astonishing was that Other Jake was not just responding to one answer; he was responding to all the answers. His arm and hand moved across the board like lightning, sketching images and math formulae to help explain his thinking.

In less than a minute Other Jake had completely filled the chalkboard. He looked at the chalk in his hand, which had been worn down to a tiny nub. Then he placed it back into the box on the ledge and turned to Mr. Glick.

"There. How is that?"

Other Jake could see the confused looks from members of his classroom. He seemed to be looking at everyone in the class except Jonathan.

Mr. Glick went to his desk and grabbed the teacher's guide from a pile of books. He scanned the answers on the board and his teacher's guide as the seconds on the classroom clock crawled by. Eventually he blinked in Other Jake's direction. "It's perfect," he said.

Now Other Jake smiled. "Of course it is. This math is so basic I could do it in my sleep."

Other Jake moved back to his seat. He didn't seem at all fazed by the weird looks he was getting from the rest of his peers. Not even Darryl Richter. "Your nose is looking a bit brown there, eh, Jake?"

Other Jake rubbed his nose and inspected his hand.

"I don't see what you mean."

Darryl leaned toward him. "I'll show you what I mean later," he said.

"Sure thing." Other Jake smiled.

Sometime later, the morning recess bell rang. Students started piling out of the room. Jonathan intended to flow out with the crowd, away from Other Jake. He'd hoped to take time to find out if Jake's eye had learned anything about Other Jake's plans. But Other Jake knew about the eye now. Jonathan couldn't risk a chance encounter between the eye, himself, and Other Jake. Instead, he planned to stay close with whatever teacher was on duty. Nothing would happen to him in plain view of everyone else.

At least for now he would be safe.

"Jonathan, do you mind staying here a moment?"

Jonathan stopped in his tracks, and turned to find Mr. Glick staring at him from his desk.

Jonathan gulped. "Uh, sure thing, Mr. Glick."

Jonathan watched Other Jake leave the room with the rest of the students. Other Jake stopped in the doorway. His gaze lingered in Jonathan's direction until he was approached by Darryl, Horace, and Malcolm by the door. "Come on, Jake."

Other Jake turned to Darryl. "Come on where?"

"We want to show you something."

"Oh," Other Jake said, his attention diverted by the bullies. "Is it interesting?"

Darryl turned to his cronies and shrugged. "Sure. It's very interesting."

Other Jake smiled his creepy smile and followed them. Jonathan didn't want anything happening to Darryl, but at least Other Jake was taken care of for the next little bit. Other Jake wasn't going to risk anything by attacking bullies during recess. At least, that's what Jonathan hoped.

Only Jonathan and Mr. Glick were left in the room now. Mr. Glick sat at his desk, going through some papers. He put them down and stared at Jonathan. "Come here."

Jonathan's knees felt shaky as he made his way to the front of the class. Mr. Glick had obviously seen Jonathan this morning. He *knew*. Why else would he ask Jonathan to stay back?

What would Mr. Glick do to him?

"You wanted to see me?" Jonathan managed.

Mr. Glick fixed Jonathan with a stare. "How are you feeling, Jonathan?"

"Uh, fine."

Mr. Glick nodded. "Of course, I'd expect you to say that. But I just get this feeling that you're — how can I put it?— *uneasy*."

He knew, all right. Now he was just playing with Jonathan, trying to make him confess. Jonathan shook his head. "I'm fine. Really —"

Out of the corner of his eye, Jonathan saw movement from the direction of the windowsill. Jake's eye was up in the air, hovering, trying to move past Jonathan and behind Mr. Glick.

Jonathan had to keep Glick stalled now, so he wouldn't turn around.

"You've been avoiding Jake the last day or so. I've noticed. *I'm good at noticing things.*"

Jonathan shivered. What else had Glick noticed? Jonathan escaping from the room? The real Jake's eye moving past him, right now, as he spoke?

Jonathan wanted to ask him all sorts of questions, like why he hadn't aged in years, but the stupider Jonathan played things, the better. It was important that whatever Mr. Glick's secrets were, Jonathan appeared to know nothing about them.

The eye had nearly reached the door out of the classroom.

"No. Everything's good, Mr. Glick." But Jonathan was having trouble showing it. He started to sweat. His heartbeat was racing. Plus, he kept swallowing nervously. How could Mr. Glick *not* notice a thing like that?

Glick narrowed his eyes. "Are you even listening to me?"

Jonathan gulped. Mr. Glick whipped his head around, looking in the direction of the door.

The eye slipped outside, into the hallway. Had Glick seen? Jonathan gulped again.

Mr. Glick turned to face Jonathan. "Tell you what," Mr. Glick smiled, changing his tone. "You go out for recess. Take a break."

Jonathan nodded. "That sounds like a great idea," he returned, trying to seem as calm as can be.

"I'll keep an eye on you." Mr. Glick smiled.

Jonathan felt sick to his stomach.

He walked outside to the hall, half wondering whether or not he was going to puke his guts out then and there from his nerves. If he was going to puke, better that he do it into a toilet.

Jonathan headed for the bathroom, but stopped in his tracks as Other Jake emerged from the entrance. Jonathan ducked behind the wall supporting the coat rack before Jake saw him. Only after he'd given enough time for Other Jake to leave the hall did Jonathan step away from the coat rack. He peered around the bend, down the hallway, then followed a bunch of third-graders outside.

He suddenly remembered Darryl Richter had asked Other Jake to follow him. Jonathan wondered why Darryl hadn't left the bathroom, and began to get ideas. Most of the ideas involved Other Jake, his teeth, and Darryl Richter in a gruesome pile of human remains on the floor.

It was totally irrational, wasn't it?

Jonathan held his breath. Darryl Richter *still* hadn't come out of the bathroom.

"Gak," Jonathan croaked. He was going to have to take a look.

Once inside, Jonathan let out a sigh of relief. Darryl Richter was standing by the mirror, slicking his hair back with water. He glanced over in Jonathan's direction. "What are you staring at, dweeb?"

"Watch yourself around him," Jonathan cautioned.

Darryl let out a hearty chortle. "Watch myself? Who are you? My mother?"

Jonathan didn't want to spend any more time around Darryl Richter than he had to, but if Darryl was going to annoy Other Jake, he had to be warned. He looked up to the ceiling, as if that might help explain things to Richter. Why did the truth have to sound so crazy? "That isn't Jake," Jonathan breathed.

"Who is it, then? Jake's evil twin brother?"

"Twin, no. Evil, yes."

Darryl made a face. "Look here. Do you remember the wedgie I gave you back in February? Do you want seconds?"

Jonathan remembered the wedgie. He did not want seconds.

"I know it sounds crazy, but —"

"I don't know what you're trying to pull," Darryl snapped, "but you're making me miss recess. Now get out of my way, and ..."

Darryl suddenly shut up.

Jonathan wasn't sure what stopped Darryl talking. Nor did he understand the sudden change of expression on Darryl's face. The furrowed brow pulled back. Then the eyes widened. Then the mouth stretched out. Finally, Jonathan recognized the expression. Darryl was afraid.

Jonathan turned.

Floating a few feet behind him was the eye. It had found its way into the boys' bathroom. How it intended to use a toilet was beyond Jonathan's understanding.

Darryl gave the kind of shrill scream that seemed more appropriate coming from a wounded bird. Secretly, Jonathan wished he could record the sound and share it with others.

After he stopped screaming, Darryl hurled himself into one of the bathroom stalls. His knee hit the side of the toilet bowl, and he fell down into a heap. It was a shame that the stall floor was wet. It was an even greater shame that not all of it was water.

The eye moved in closer. The pupil flashed angrily. Darryl scrambled to get away, and accidentally flushed the toilet trying to get up. "That's impossible!" he yelped.

Jonathan stepped into the stall. "What's impossible?"

He was enjoying this moment, and tried to draw it out as long as possible.

"That's the thing that gave me the black eye!"

"What? This eye ... gave you a black eye?"

"Shut up! I don't want to talk about it! Just get it away from me!"

The eye looked from Darryl to Jonathan, and back again. Jonathan dug a hand into his pocket and produced the jar. "Come on, Jake. Show's over."

Darryl made a face. "Jake?"

"You heard me."

"The floating eye is called Jake?"

"It's Jake's eye, yep."

Darryl shook his head, desperately trying to make sense of this. "Jake is outside."

"No," Jonathan returned. "That's Other Jake. At least, that's what I'm calling him for now. He's not even human."

Darryl heard the words, but he wasn't making sense of them. His head spun. The whole world spun. All he could focus on was the eye. That thing had entered his room. He'd been hit on the head. It wanted to hurt him. "Get it out of here," Darryl hissed.

Jonathan turned to the eye and waved the jar. "Let's go. Get inside."

Begrudgingly, the eye obeyed. Jonathan screwed the cap on the jar and stuck it in his pocket. Then he leaned over and helped Darryl to his feet. "You're going to need to wash your pants," he said.

Darryl had other things on his mind. "What is going on? I want the truth." Darryl tried to use his bully voice to get the edge in the conversation, but it was useless. Jonathan held all the cards.

"That eye is all that's left of the Jake that you and I know. The rest of him is stuck back at that cemetery you and your idiot friends tripped us up at."

"Stuck how?" Darryl didn't necessarily believe Jonathan, but at least he was getting answers.

"He's trapped in a tombstone. Except it's not a tombstone. The thing that was trapped inside of it has shape-shifted into what appears to be Jake. Believe me, it's not."

"You've been watching too many horror movies," Darryl said.

"Darryl, I can't do this alone. I need to stop Other Jake. I need to get something from him. And then I need to get Other Jake back to that cemetery, so I can switch him up for the real Jake." Jonathan took a moment to catch his breath, all the while looking Darryl Richter straight in the eye. "Are you with me?"

Darryl considered this very carefully.

"Will I get to give Jake a wedgie?"

"As long as it's to Other Jake."

The recess bell rang, echoing through the bathroom.

"Okay," Darryl said. "I'm in."

Darryl narrowed his eyes for a moment.

"What?" Jonathan asked.

"I was just thinking. If Other Jake sees us walking out of here together, he's going to figure something's up."

"But Other Jake is already outside."

"How do you know for sure?" Darryl tried.

"Okay," Jonathan huffed, "I get it. We have to keep this thing between us a secret. What do you suggest?"

"I'll leave first."

"Okay."

"But we're going to have to make this look convincing."

Now it was Jonathan's turn to narrow his eyes. "How?"

Darryl smiled. "Well, under normal circumstances, I'd be giving *you* a wedgie right now."

Jonathan was about to protest, but if Other Jake *did* see them leaving together, he might suspect something was up. Jonathan fumed. He pulled the jar containing the eye out of his pocket and glared at it. "Don't say I'm not taking one for the team!" he spat, then put the jar down on the ground.

The eye watched, unblinking, as Darryl got to work.

The wedgie had been a good one. Darryl had seen to that.

So Jonathan waddled back into the classroom looking like a grumpy penguin. He was forced to pull the wedgie out in front of half the girls in class, including Lindsay.

"That's disgusting!" she exclaimed, turning away. "You are the grossest person alive, Jonathan!"

The attention roused Other Jake's interest, too. "Your underwear appears to be stretched beyond its means," he noted.

"Thanks," Jonathan returned. "I noticed."

"Is that how people are wearing it these days?"

Jonathan badly wanted to show Other Jake what it would be like to wear his underwear so high you could mistake it for a shirt, but Darryl sidled into view and clamped an arm around Other Jake's shoulder. "Want me to show you?" he asked Other Jake.

Other Jake looked from the pained expression on Jonathan's face to the gleam in Darryl Richter's eye. "Perhaps some other time," he suggested, and moved aside.

"I'll pencil you in," Darryl returned.

As Other Jake walked into class, Darryl grabbed a hold of Jonathan's shoulder and yanked him back. "Nice work, huh?"

"Yeah," Jonathan huffed, pulling the last of his wedgie out. "You did great."

"So what's the plan?" Darryl asked.

"Other Jake has the core that will set the real Jake free. We need to get it from him. We'll go to the real Jake's house after school. That thing is obviously keeping his secrets there."

Darryl smiled. "*Break in*, you mean? I like breaking into things. And breaking things."

Jonathan nodded knowingly.

The sky was the colour of dying embers as the sun dipped below the horizon. As shadows began to cloak the streets, Jonathan found Darryl by the big oak tree a few doors down from Jake's house. Years ago, Jonathan had dared Jake to try climbing the tree. Jake had gotten only a few feet, but Jonathan had reached the first limb. That was as far as he'd gotten. Jonathan fell right onto the sidewalk, cracking one of his ribs in the process. Boy, had that hurt!

The tree served to remind Jonathan that what he and Darryl were doing was dangerous. But if they didn't try to stop Other Jake now, when would they? Other Jake was up to something. He'd been collecting bits and pieces of machinery, and it was time to find out why.

Darryl was dressed in a dark tracksuit and wore a hoodie to keep his face shielded. He'd obviously done this sort of thing before. Or, at the very least, had seen a lot of TV shows in which people broke into houses. Jonathan guessed it was the latter, judging by the uneasy way Darryl looked around.

"Are you sure this is a good idea?" Darryl said nervously. "What if we, you know, get caught?"

"I thought you liked breaking into things," Jonathan stated.

Darryl glanced over his shoulder. He leaned in close to Jonathan and whispered, "That's just talk. I've never broken into anything."

"Oh," Jonathan said, trying to pretend that this was actual news to him. Jonathan had begun to realize that there was a little less to Darryl than met the eye.

Darryl narrowed his eyes. "But if you let anybody know about that, I'll break you."

"I'm sure you will," Jonathan said dismissively, then dug into his pocket for the phone. He punched in Jake's phone number and waited for the ring.

"Hello, friend," came the answer. The voice, which sounded exactly like Jake's, made Jonathan shiver.

"I want to meet with you," Jonathan said flatly, "to discuss business."

"Business?"

"Whatever it is you're doing, I want to help."

"Is that so?"

"Yeah, it is," Jonathan said. He tried his best to sound brave. It was hard when his hand was shaking so much with fear that he could barely keep the phone cradled to his ear. A car whizzed past him.

"Where are you?" Other Jake asked.

"The park by my place. Meet me there in twenty minutes."

There was a pause on the other end of the line. "I look forward to our meeting," Other Jake returned. "I am most curious about this business of ours."

The line went dead.

Jonathan lowered the phone and let out a shaky sigh. "I just bought us, like, forty minutes," he said. "Now we hide."

Darryl shifted his weight from foot to foot. "What about Jake's parents? Won't they be at home?"

Jonathan shook his head. "They go to yoga class together tonight," he replied. "Normally, tonight's the night I go to Jake's and watch scary movies."

"This *is* a scary movie," Darryl returned.

The boys waited five minutes before heading over to Jake's house. One of the lights had been left on, but that wasn't news. Jake's family always left the lights on when they went out, to deter burglars. The light did nothing to deter Jonathan and Darryl from getting a closer look.

"How do we, you know, do it?" Darryl asked, when they reached the back door.

Jonathan turned to see Darryl standing there. He was holding a big rock he'd plucked from the garden. "I've never broken a window in. You think there's a special way to smash it?"

Jonathan rolled his eyes. "When I said break in, I didn't mean literally. Jake told me where his parents keep the spare key years ago."

"Oh," Darryl said. He dropped the rock.

Jonathan shook his head, knelt down beside the potted plant near the back door, and lifted it. "Ta-dah!!!"

"You lifted a plant," Darryl observed.

Jonathan leaned closer. "It's not there," he said, patting the ground. "You might want to pick up that rock after all."

"Uh, Jonathan …"

"I know, I know. There's a sign in the window saying the house is protected by some fancy security company, but it's not. That's just there to scare burglars away."

"Jonathan …"

Jonathan was still fishing around in the dark, trying to find the key. Maybe it had fallen on the ground? "That key's gotta be around here somewhere …"

"I don't think we're going to need it," Darryl said.

"And why's that?"

"Because Jake's standing right behind you."

Jonathan turned around to find that Other Jake was indeed standing right there, with a curious look on his face. "I thought you wanted to meet at the park."

Jonathan got to his feet. In the dark, it was hard to see how much colour had drained from his face.

"Jake!" Jonathan tried to smile, as if this were all part of the scheme. "There's been a slight change of plans."

"I know." Other Jake smiled. "Why don't you come with me? I have something to show you."

CHAPTER 13

Other Jake led the two boys away from the backyard, past the house, and down to the garage at the foot of the property.

"Why are we going here?"

Other Jake regarded Jonathan and Darryl as if they were a pair of idiots. "How many times have you been to this place?"

"A bunch?" Jonathan tried.

Other Jake nodded. "And in that time, have you ever gone into the garage?"

Jonathan said nothing. He'd been over countless times to hang out with Jake, and never set foot in the place. The garage wasn't exactly off-limits; it was just a place nobody bothered about. Even the cars didn't make it into the garage. They were always left outside.

Other Jake plucked a key from his pocket and opened the garage door. He motioned for the two to follow.

Jonathan's attention was immediately taken by what lay on the workbench. Other Jake had cannibalized his desktop computer for various parts. He'd also brought in other electronics and taken them to pieces, too. The resulting sculpture on the workshop desk — a mass of wires, circuits, mother-boards, and flashing LED lights — looked extremely deli-cate. "What is all this stuff?" he asked.

Other Jake sidled into view. "What do you think?"

Jonathan turned to Darryl and shrugged. "Looks great," he said, matter-of-factly.

"Do you know what it does?" Other Jake asked, main-taining perfect posture and his ever-present smile. If you could get past the teeth and the threats and the fact that real Jake was still stuck in the tombstone, Other Jake had his share of eerie charm.

"It does your math homework for you," Jonathan sug-gested.

Other Jake shook his head. "Shall I show you?"

Other Jake flipped a switch. The LED lights began to flash on and off with alarming speed. A bicycle wheel that had been turned on its side and mounted on an old record player began to spin. It turned a series of gears that were con-nected by wires to the assembled computer motherboards. Jonathan tried to follow the mechanical workings of the ma-chine, but soon all manner of household objects were spin-ning, grinding, turning. What appeared to be junk or refuse strewn about the room began to move in accordance with the machine.

"What is it?" Darryl gasped.

"It's a signalling device," Other Jake beamed.

"What's it signalling?"

"My friends. My *good* friends," Other Jake corrected himself.

"What? We're not your friends?" Darryl tried weak-ly. Who was he kidding, he thought to himself. Did he really think anyone would believe he could be Jake's friend? He'd been absolutely horrible to Real Jake. The things he'd done over the last few years ... why hadn't anyone stopped him? Why not Malcolm or Horace? They'd just been standing around him, hadn't they? Feeding off his little ego trips. All at Jake's expense. Everything he'd built himself up to be, all that coolness and power, it was all by putting other people down.

Darryl shuddered. People didn't like him. They were afraid of him. They laughed at his jokes because they had to. They moved out of his way because they feared what he might do if they didn't.

But this Jake — this Other Jake — he didn't fear Darryl. He looked as if he didn't fear anything. And because he had no fear, he could do whatever he wanted. Looking at Other Jake, Darryl felt as if he was standing in front of a mirror. Only that mirror didn't reflect his image, but his effect on others. Finally Darryl understood, and felt a sinking in the pit of his stomach. How awful had he been? And how could he find a way out of it?

Jonathan, meanwhile, had been focusing on something else. "Aliens," he said. He hadn't used the word before. The floating eye, the cemetery, the possessed hand. It had seemed like the stuff from a horror movie, something supernatural. The idea of aliens hadn't entered his head until now.

"As far as I'm concerned, this world of yours is alien," Other Jake said. "But it will suit our purposes quite adequately."

"Our purposes?" Jonathan asked. His eyes darted about the room, trying to search for a means of stopping the machine.

147

"The ship that crashed behind your cemetery? The core? What do you think that little piece of stone was?"

"A core?" Jonathan tried.

Other Jake dug into his pocket and pulled out the core. He let it roll around in his palm and felt the weight of it. How many years had he spent stuck in that hellish trap? It felt like millennia. An eternity of waiting in agonizing stasis. That was over now. Soon, others would come. They would feast. And they would take this world by storm.

"A key," Other Jake corrected. "It unlocks the prison I've been trapped in for …" Other Jake stopped and turned to a computer monitor behind him. He put the core down onto the table and hit a few keys to read some numbers off the screen. "… one hundred eighty-three years? How time flies."

Jonathan's eyes remained locked on the core.

"See something you like?"

Jonathan looked back up to find Other Jake staring him down.

"You don't look a day over twelve," Jonathan admitted.

Other Jake grinned. "You're funny. Jake likes that about you, you know."

"You can read his mind?"

"I absorb all sorts of information when I body-shift. Just as my friends will absorb all there is to know about you."

This was bad. Really, extremely bad. It was the kind of situation that required quick thinking and immediate action. It was the sort of situation Darryl would be able to help with. Jonathan turned to Darryl. Then he mouthed one word: "Wedgie."

Darryl smiled.

Without warning, the two of them rushed at Other Jake.

148

Darryl latched onto the backside of Other Jake's pants and yanked as hard as he could.

The sinister smile on Other Jake's face vanished. There was a look of surprise, of being caught off guard, but only for a moment. A new expression overtook Other Jake's face, one that neither Darryl nor Jonathan had seen before.

Anger.

Darryl had never ticked off a space alien before. He had no idea what to expect.

For one thing, a shape-shifting alien doesn't necessarily feel pain in the same way or place as a human does.

As Darryl yanked Other Jake's pants, he found that Other Jake's underwear was riding way too far up the crotch. In fact, the wedgie was pulling right *through* Other Jake, tearing him in half up the middle.

The two halves of Other Jake fell to the ground, each limb kicking. The head had also been sliced in half. The creature let out a low, inhuman moan. Air bubbles oozed up from the tarry substance that leaked out of the creature's body.

Darryl screamed.

The two halves of Other Jake flailed about on the floor, one half of the head staring at Jonathan, the other at Darryl. Both eyes boiled in fury. The creature let out a high-pitched squeal that rattled the windows.

The creature's insides were composed of a churning, dark substance that poured across the floor to rejoin with the other half of itself. The two pools of liquid ran into each other, and the two halves of the creature were pulled together. The split joined back together again, into the familiar form of Jake.

Jonathan and Darryl could only stand, frozen in horror.

The creature picked itself up off the floor and stared at the two boys through eyes that kept flickering from human to alien. They rolled in their sockets, like the dials of a slot machine. Eventually they settled on a pair that resembled Jake's.

Then it opened its mouth so wide that Other Jake's head seemed to flip directly off the jawbone. A deep gurgle rumbled out from the creature's stomach. It gargled up a thick, phlegm-like substance and sprayed it at the boys.

It spattered against Darryl and Jonathan's legs and feet and formed a thick, goopy puddle on the floor.

Normally, this sort of startling action would cause somebody to jump back in shock. Darryl and Jonathan tried, but they couldn't move. The thick substance had hardened and locked them into place.

They could only watch helplessly as the creature closed its head, which now looked as Real Jake's should have, and stared at them. It was not smiling.

"Nice try," Other Jake said. "Now if you'll excuse me, I've got to finish readying the signalling device. See you in a few." Other Jake turned and made his way to the door.

"What are you going to do to us?" Jonathan asked.

Other Jake stopped. He took a step closer. "Like I said, my real friends will be here soon. They'll have been travelling for some time." Other Jake licked his lips. "They'll be *hungry*."

With that, Other Jake turned and stormed outside. He slammed the door behind him, leaving the two boys stuck in the middle of the garage.

Darryl let out a shaky breath. "Think we should try shouting for help?"

"Who's going to hear us out here? The garage isn't even

attached to the house."

"What do you suggest?"

"Look," Jonathan said, and pointed to the workbench.

In his anger, Other Jake must have forgotten that he'd set the core down beside the computer. All Jonathan had to do was grab it, find a way to unstick himself and Darryl, and then stop the creature. The trouble was the grabbing part. The table was too far away to reach.

Darryl was bent over, scanning the ground around them. Not too far away was a hockey stick. If he could grab hold of that, reach over to the table —

No. Also out of reach.

The only thing in his grasp was an old baseball. He picked it up and tossed it up and down in his hand. "I could whip this off the wall, maybe knock the core from the table …"

"Too risky," Jonathan said.

"So what do we do?"

Jonathan pursed his lips. "I'm thinking," he muttered.

Darryl caught sight of Jake's house through the window. One of the bedroom lights was on. Darryl squinted and made out the form of Other Jake gathering some stuff. "Better think quickly. We're almost out of time."

Darryl tightened his grip on the softball. "I could throw this at his invention."

"You could, but then we'd still be stuck here. And Other Jake will just get angrier."

"You sound like you're giving up."

Jonathan huffed. "I can't see how we're going to get out of this one," he admitted. If Other Jake brought others down to this world, what chance did Jonathan and Darryl stand?

Other Jake wasn't going to let them go. Jonathan's face was red. His eyes began to water. Panic began to overtake him. For once, there didn't seem to be any way out of this. "Nobody else knows we're here," Jonathan sniffed.

Jonathan was wrong.

CHAPTER 14

Jake had been trapped in his prison under the ground for nearly two days now, although as far as he was concerned, it might have been forever. The only concept of time passing came from what the eye could see.

He remembered how he got here. The creature had attacked him so suddenly that he was unable to escape in time. He remembered the feeling of his arms and legs being locked into position, and the solid tombstone melting into liquid around him.

The melting stone had reached his face. He'd opened his mouth to scream, but that just gave the liquefying tombstone more places to ooze into. It had run down his throat, into his stomach, racing into his intestines and who knows where else? It had flooded into his nostrils, suffocating him. Any part of his body that had air in it had been filled with this alien substance that immediately hardened like cement.

His body ached and his muscles burned. The solidified goop that invaded his body held him stiff as a board.

He was trapped, but he could still feel. Still itch. Still ache. Although his lungs did not need to hold breath, they still yearned for it. The tombstone's material hadn't conked out Jake's nerves. Now that he couldn't move, his senses were all heightened. All he felt was agony.

Jake had seen flies and other prehistoric insects trapped in hunks of amber. That's just what he was now, an insect trapped with no apparent means of escape.

Jake thought the insects had it pretty easy. At least they'd died. They didn't have to go on living, trapped and unable to move. Jake was burdened with the awareness that he was stuck. Claustrophobia took hold. How many hours had Jake been encased in the stone, trying to scream with lungs that were filled with something thick and cold?

He hadn't died. That was strange. As far as he understood, he needed air to breathe, water to drink, and food to eat, but whatever substance had trapped him provided what was needed to stay alive. He simply had to endure the torture of being aware he was stuck, unable to move, or even blink.

Yet able to see.

The creature had turned its back, confident that Jake would not escape. Maybe Jake couldn't escape, but his eye could.

Yes, that was one power Jake still had. He could see, and he could move. Even if he couldn't do a thing with the rest of his body, his lone eye had escaped.

It happened so suddenly and quickly that Jake had hardly known it himself. Just as he'd been forced into the alien prison, the one part of his body that *could* escape took the opportunity.

When his eye had first left its socket in the middle of the night, just a few days back, Jake had thought it was a dream. Then he saw what was happening, and it terrified him. There should be no way to control an eye to make it float.

Only after ejecting his eye from its socket when the creature had thrown him in here had Jake finally understood.

It was hard to explain, but there was something about the actual stone he was trapped in that made it work. On the one hand, the stone was keeping his body locked into place. But the stone had other properties: it could affect anything it touched. Maybe that's why Jake had found the stone surrounded by a circle of dead grass — the creature inside had killed it, maybe tried sucking the nutrition out of it.

There was a small piece of the stone embedded in his eye. It must have gotten in there when Jake had scratched it on the tombstone, just as it had with Shawn Crumb's eye. That was all that was needed. Although Jake's other senses were cut off or unable to do anything, he immediately had the mental image of what the other eye saw.

He had the ability to see when the creature had been controlling the eye, too. Only now, Jake was in control. All he had to do was think about moving the eye up, and the eye obeyed. With his other senses cut off, Jake could focus on how to work the eye. Every detail jumped out at him with incredible clarity. Jake had heard about blind people whose other senses seemed heightened. This was like the reverse. He couldn't hear, taste, or smell, but with his lone eye, he could see better than ever before. With only the eye to experience things outside his new prison, it suddenly became a vast looking glass to the world, one that he could control with the slightest thought.

He had found his way to Jonathan's house and bounced the eye against the window. Sure, it had hurt plenty, because he still had the nerve endings in his body to feel pain with, but it had gotten Jonathan's attention. It was good to see his friend again. Luckily Jonathan had understood how to communicate by setting up a system of questions that could be answered with yes or no.

It had been fun scaring the heck out of Darryl Richter too. Jake wondered if it was almost worth getting himself locked up in the tombstone for, but this could well be for eternity, and he hadn't even gotten the satisfaction of hearing Darryl scream.

Now the last thing Jake ever expected had happened! Darryl was on his side. He wondered, if this somehow ended well (if Jonathan and Darryl didn't get chomped or killed by the Thing), whether he and Darryl could smooth things out.

Before any of that could happen, Jake had to stop the creature.

Jonathan and Darryl were trapped in the goop, which this impostor had vomited up at them. They had no means of pulling themselves free. They were stuck.

Jake's parents never used the garage for anything but a storage shed. They'd piled all sorts of stuff there they hadn't bothered to throw out. Cut off from the house, the garage was a safe haven for anyone wanting to hide something or experiment unseen by others.

Nobody else knew about the impostor. Jonathan and Darryl could try to explain, but without proof, who would believe it? Now Jake was alone. Only he could stop this.

Deep inside the tombstone, Jake struggled, but he could not move one muscle, nor gasp one breath. There was nothing he could do.

Only the eye could.

The eye hung outside the window and stared into the room.

Jonathan and Darryl were helpless. The impostor had gone back into the house to work on something, leaving them stranded.

What could Jake do?

Jonathan and Darryl had already tried to steal the core, trap the impostor, and bring him back to the cemetery to switch the thing up with Jake. They'd failed.

If only Jake could somehow free himself. Then he could lure his double back to the cemetery and perhaps find a way to put it back into the tombstone. He'd need the core to do that. Making matters worse was the fact that the core was sitting on the table, out of arm's reach for Jonathan and Darryl. The core seemed to be taunting them to make a grab for it, but the table was too far away.

Jonathan and Darryl were helpless. They were stuck there. They were —

Stuck!

The eye's pupil widened.

Stuck. That was it. The eye couldn't pick anything up, but if it could somehow *stick* something to it, it might be able to grab the core and make an escape with it.

The garage window was shut, and so was the door. However, there was a tiny gap near the bottom. Jake manoeuvred the eye down to the base of the garage door and squeezed inside.

A moment later, the eye was hovering in front of the two boys. Through it, Jake saw the excited looks on their faces, even Darryl's, and saw their mouths move. The eye could not hear what was being said. There was no time to waste.

Jake had a plan. He moved the eye to the sink.

The taps on the garage sink were the old-fashioned kind, with projectile spokes. Some of the newer faucets had little knobs to turn the water on with. Thankfully, Jake's garage did not.

Jake currently had no hands to turn the tap on with. All he could do was wedge the eye in between the spokes of the hot water tap and push. The metal of the spoke pressed against his naked eye.

Deep in the tombstone, Jake tried to blink away the irritation in his eye. It was agonizing.

Push!

The pain in his eye was tremendous. Had the eye been in his head, he'd be on the floor in tears by now. Now the pain seemed to fuel him. Let it hurt. Let it be excruciating. If pain was the one thing he could feel right now, at least it reminded Jake he was still alive.

The tap began to open.

A thin stream of water trickled out.

Jake pushed the eye harder.

The stream of water grew stronger. Soon, the faucet began to heat up. Now it wasn't just a pressure against Jake's eye, but heat surrounding it as well.

Jake pushed until he couldn't stand the pain. He moved the eye away from the tap to regard his handiwork.

A cloud of steam rose from the sink and began to fog up the window.

Perfect!

Now he just had to write his message.

Jake didn't have the world's greatest penmanship. Thankfully, he didn't have to write much. One word would do, in fact.

Jake got to work. Because the eye was pressed up against the window, Jake was too close to see what he was writing. He concentrated on the letters and wiped them across the window. Just three letters would do it. Satisfied that he had achieved his goal, Jake piloted the eye away and regarded his handiwork.

The three letters spelled GUM.

The eye turned to Darryl and Jonathan. "Gum?" they mouthed together.

The eye tried to nod. Then the eye flew to the core sitting on the table, and back to the word GUM.

Only this time, Jake's eye got a good look through the letters on the window.

Other Jake was standing right outside.

He could see the word written on the window, and he could see the eye.

CHAPTER 15

Jake flew the eye away from the window and over to the side door by the garage. The doorknob had a protruding button that locked it.

The knob twisted as Other Jake made a move to open it.

Jake rammed the eye at the button at full speed, jamming it into place.

The doorknob rattled back and forth violently, clearly locked. Next, Other Jake started to pound at the door.

The eye moved back to Darryl and Jonathan, who were now staring at the door wide-eyed.

The eye moved in on Darryl, thumping against his pants pocket.

Darryl tore his gaze from the door and stared down at the eye. He dug into his pocket and pulled out a pack of bubble gum. He looked at the eye. "You want me to chew gum at a time like this? Man, get your priorities straight!"

Other Jake continued to pound on the door.

"Hang on," Jonathan said. "Let's put this together. We've got gum. There's the core. And there's the eye."

"I don't see how this helps us."

"We'll stick the gum to the eye. The eye can get to the core."

"And then what?"

The sound of pounding on the garage door suddenly stopped.

There was a reason Other Jake had stopped, Darryl was certain of it. He narrowed his eyes as an uneasy idea entered his head. "Hey, where does Jake keep the clicker to open the garage door?"

"I don't know. Inside a car?"

"Chew!" Darryl yelped, wedging two pieces of gum into his mouth. "Chew like your life depends on it!"

"But my life does depend on it."

"Then you won't need much convincing!" Darryl tossed the rest of the pack of gum to Jonathan, and chewed madly.

They both did.

It only took a minute to work the gum into a dripping, sticky wad. Jonathan passed his to Darryl and wiped his mouth.

The eye floated over to Darryl and watched him combine the two pieces of chewed gum together.

"This is mostly disgusting," Darryl said. He had to hold the eye in his hands and stick the gum to the bottom of it. The eye kept slipping around in his fingers, like a bar of wet soap.

"No, not that way," Jonathan tried. "The core is too heavy. If Jake tries to lift up the core with the eye, the gum will just fall off. You've got to roll the gum into a ball and stick the eye inside. That's the only way."

Darryl looked at Jonathan. "Like I said, this is mostly disgusting." He rolled the wad of gum into a ball. He took

161

Jake's eye and twisted it in so the eye held there. Then he let go.

The eye, now trailing a thick stringy wad of gum, moved over to the core.

It was a long shot. Would it work?

Jake plopped the eye down onto the core, then slowly floated back up.

The gum stretched into thin strands as it struggled with the weight.

Darryl and Jonathan watched with bated breath as the conical core lifted away from the table.

The eye moved back to Jonathan, who went to work wrapping the gum around the core so it would stay stuck to the eye.

A sudden tremor shook the garage walls. A loud hum filled the room. The garage door slowly opened to reveal Other Jake standing there, the clicker in his hand.

Seeing the eye and core wrapped up in gum, Other Jake dropped the clicker and made a wild grab for the core. The eye darted out of reach, but Other Jake leapt up and smacked the eye and the core down to the concrete floor of the garage.

Other Jake reared up to pounce on the eye.

Darryl, still clutching the baseball, wound up. "Hey, Other Jake!" he shouted.

Other Jake looked up in time to see Darryl fire the ball right at his head.

The impact knocked Other Jake off his feet, sending him skidding against the pavement.

"Steeee-rike!" Jonathan yelped.

For a second, Other Jake just lay there. Then he sat up, and Jonathan jumped.

The baseball was stuck in Other Jake's head. It had smashed a crater into his nose. No bones appeared to be broken. It was as if Other Jake's head had caved in. Now Other Jake sucked in a breath of air. He blew it out through his mouth and nostrils, forcing the baseball to pop out of his face. Other Jake continued to inhale and exhale, forcing his face back into a shape that once again approximated Real Jake's head.

Other Jake was still re-inflating his head as the eye floated back up into the air with the core and sped off through the open garage door, into the night. He turned in the direction of the core, then whipped his head around to glower at the two boys. Other Jake snarled at them, dog-like, then leapt to his feet and dashed outside.

He didn't chase the eye, however. He stopped at Jake's dad's car in the driveway and punched his fist through the driver's side window.

Shards of safety glass rained down onto the driveway. Other Jake reached his hand into the car and opened the lock. He tore the door open and slipped inside. For a second, it looked as if he was raising his hand to wave good-bye to Jonathan and Darryl. Instead, Other Jake's hand shimmered and ran, shifting form. His index finger took on the shape of a car key, and he jammed his hand into the ignition and cranked it.

The car rumbled to life. Headlights snapped on, nearly blinding Jonathan and Darryl. Tires squealed as Other Jake stuck the car into reverse and peeled out of the driveway. The car hopped the curb, throwing sparks, and taking out the garbage can that had been placed there. Other Jake threw the vehicle into drive and tore off down the road. The garbage can rolled across the street, spilling trash everywhere.

"That guy's never going to get a driver's license," Jonathan noted.

Several lights went on in neighbouring houses. A moment later, people began to spill out into their front yards. So did Jake's parents. They came running to the front of the driveway to find the two boys stuck in place.

"Jonathan? What's going on?" Jake's mom asked.

"Where's my car?!" Jake's dad blurted. He stopped and looked at the shattered glass littering the driveway and began to do the math. Even in the dim light, one could see the colour drain from his face.

"Where's Jake?" Jake's dad asked, growing more frantic by the second.

"He's … not here," Jonathan returned. How was he going to explain this one? There was no time to lose.

"He took the car?!" Jake's dad roared.

"No, that was *Other* Jake," Darryl returned.

"Who are you?"

"Oh, I'm Darryl. Hi."

Jake's dad's eyes flashed pure fury at Darryl. "The bully?"

Hesitantly, Darryl nodded. *This* was what Jake's dad was going to get upset about now?

"What did you do?" he thundered.

Darryl looked around. "Hang on a sec. You think *I* had something to do with this?"

"Your name is Darryl, and you did give my son several wedgies."

Darryl's face flushed. He'd been giving Jake a hard time for so long now, he could barely remember when they were supposedly friends. Tormenting Jake wasn't what he set out to do on a daily basis, but Jake had been so easy to tease. He always got a good reaction from it. Maybe not from Jake, but that was going to change. It was kind of hard to explain that to Jake's dad, though. The guy looked about as mad as a volcano on eruption day. "When this is all done, you can give me all the wedgies you like." He caught the look from Jake's dad's eyes and winced. "*Sir.*" Now, back to business. "But we don't have time for that. Other Jake's going to catch up with Real Jake's eye, and if we don't stop him, we'll never get Other Jake back into the tombstone."

Jake's parents looked at each other dumbfounded.

"Say," Jonathan interjected, pointing to the thick wad of hardened phlegm at their feet. "You wouldn't happen to have a hacksaw or a hatchet, would you? We're kind of stuck here."

After convincing them that no, they didn't have enough time to make any phone calls, and that they knew where "Jake" was headed, Jonathan and Darryl got Jake's parents to drive them to the cemetery.

They arrived to discover Jake's parents' other car by the front gate, vacant. The two boys immediately bolted from the back seat and hopped the fence, leaving Jake's parents behind still unfastening their seat belts.

There was no time to explain.

Jonathan and Darryl raced down the hill. It didn't matter that the hill was too steep, or that they immediately lost their footing and tumbled halfway down. It didn't matter that they got cut and bruised and had to stagger the rest of the way to the tombstone that wasn't a tombstone. What mattered was that they were there to help their friend.

Jonathan had been expecting to find the eye here, but

what he found instead surprised him.

A shadowy figure was sitting on the tombstone. He looked as if he had been waiting for them to show up for some time. He was clutching the small device Jonathan had photographed earlier — small, jet black, and with two pointed ends making it look like a miniature of the tombstone he now sat on.

"What are *you* doing here?" Jonathan asked.

Mr. Glick hopped off the tombstone, took a few steps forward into the moonlight, and grinned. "Ah, I see you found my grandfather's tombstone. Remind me to give you two bonus points on the next math test."

CHAPTER 16

Darryl shook his head. There were a great many things he wanted to ask, but all he could manage was one word. He said it with absolute disbelief and conviction. "What?"

Mr. Glick smiled. "Ah, Mr. Richter. So you've come along for the outing, have you? I suppose I'll have to give you some extra points as well."

It was Jonathan's turn to shake his head in bewilderment. "What?"

"You really have to stop saying 'what' to me. It's not a question the way you use it. More like an exclamation. And it's probably not going to give you any of the answers that you're seeking."

"Fine," Jonathan stammered, and collected himself as best he could. "But, what *are* you doing here?"

Mr. Glick surveyed the surroundings, as if he was being watched, and tiptoed over to the two boys. "Waiting," he whispered secretly, then looked over his shoulder again.

Jonathan and Darryl each took a step back.

"Waiting for what?"

Mr. Glick smiled.

Somewhere behind them, a branch snapped.

And another.

Before Jonathan and Darryl could fully spin around, he was already there, standing patiently: Other Jake.

In his hand he clutched the long cylindrical core for the tombstone. Attached to the core by a piece of gum was Jake's eye.

"Good," Other Jake started, "I was hoping to find you here."

"Of course we're here," Jonathan snapped. "We chased you."

Mr. Glick cleared his throat. "I believe he was referring to *me*."

Other Jake pushed past the two boys until he stood before Mr. Glick. The two regarded each other. Mr. Glick bent down and sniffed Other Jake's ears and neck, then let out a low, guttural sound. The skin around his throat seemed to expand and contract, as if someone had glued a lung inside of it.

Other Jake handed the core to Mr. Glick.

Mr. Glick held it in his free hand and smiled a big, wide smile. A smile that was too wide for any human. He chattered his teeth madly: an incessant, clicking sound that raised the hair on Jonathan and Darryl's heads.

"You know how long I've been searching for this?" Mr. Glick said to Other Jake.

Other Jake shrugged. "How could I know? I have been in that prison for so long …"

"Well over one hundred and eighty years," Mr. Glick answered. He reached to the bottom of the core and yanked off the thick wad of pink gum, Jake's eye and all, and flung it on top of the tombstone.

"What's the big deal?" Jonathan spat fearfully. He wanted answers now.

Both Mr. Glick and Other Jake stared at the two boys.

"I get it," Jonathan said. "You're both in on this whole shape-changing alien business. But why is the core so important? Other Jake is free. You don't need it anymore."

In response, Other Jake snarled, revealing two rows of jagged teeth.

Jonathan jumped back, right into Darryl. The two of them fell to the ground in a heap.

"The core is not just a key," Glick explained. "It's a homing device. The others can finally lock onto our signal. Soon they will join us."

"Hang on," Darryl said, pulling himself off the ground. "Why are you telling us this? You know we're going to try to stop you." He turned to Jonathan. "That's what we're going to do, right?"

He helped Jonathan to his feet, and stared Other Jake down.

Behind them, Mr. Glick gently placed the core on top of the tombstone, then stepped away and moved beside Other Jake.

"*Try* being the operative word," Mr. Glick returned.

"We'll do more than try," said Jonathan. "Jake's parents are here too, and as soon as they get down here you guys are toast."

Other Jake did not take his eyes off Darryl. The two of them stood frozen, eye-to-eye, as if locked in some kind of staring contest. Darryl clenched his fist, as if to punch Other Jake. Other Jake clenched the same fist. Darryl lifted that clenched fist, to warn Other Jake away. Other Jake lifted his clenched fist at exactly the same time.

"No," Darryl and Other Jake said simultaneously.

"Stop it," Darryl and Other Jake said again, simultaneously.

Other Jake was copying his every move. Studying him. Darryl turned to Jonathan (Other Jake did, too). Darryl could see Jonathan's shocked reaction, only Jonathan wasn't looking at Darryl and Other Jake. He was staring in Mr. Glick's direction. Darryl and Other Jake followed Jonathan's gaze.

Mr. Glick had now matched Jonathan's actions, move for move.

But there was more.

Already, Other Jake's face was switching. His skin had changed colour, ever so slightly, and the bones and facial features shifted under the skin. Other Jake's hair rippled in the night air, despite the complete lack of breeze. His eyes went from blue to brown, and when Other Jake blinked (because Darryl had blinked), Darryl found himself looking at a perfect copy of himself.

"I don't believe it," Darryl and Other Darryl gasped.

"Believe it," came a familiar voice from beyond. Darryl and Other Darryl turned. Mr. Glick had vanished.

In his place stood, well, Other Jonathan.

The Jonathans turned to the Darryls.

"This is where things get a little complicated," one of the Jonathans said. Darryl wasn't sure which.

There are some things in life that you never pay close attention to, unless you happen to be a disembodied eye stuck to a big wad of gum. One of those things is the edge of a hunk of space rock disguised as a tombstone.

For a long while, Jake saw the edge of the tombstone, and nothing more.

He noticed the grain of the rock. He observed the smooth polished edge. He got a really good view of a blob of bird droppings, which were right in front of him. Jake tried to focus his eye from the bird droppings to the polished edge. He hoped that he might catch a glimpse of the reflection of his two best friends in that reflection. All he got was a blur.

What Jake couldn't see well was the struggle between the Darryls and Jonathans. The eye was still stuck in the wad of gum, and that was smeared across the tombstone.

Deep within the prison beneath the tombstone, Jake concentrated. He forced himself to focus on levitating the eye and pushing it free of the gum.

But the eye, like his body, was trapped. He only managed to wiggle it a little bit forward, so that the eye rolled over the bird poop and came to a sticky stop. Now he could see nothing but a disgusting white smear. He couldn't even hear the sound of struggling. For all he knew, this was it. Jonathan and Darryl were at the mercy of those two monsters, and soon they would be dead.

Jake wasn't sure how much time passed before he noticed something.

The ground around him was starting to tremble.

Soon the trembling shifted into a full-blown rumble. It felt like a jet airplane was taking off from deep underground, and Jake was wedged right in the engine.

Was that it? Was he actually taking off? Had this tombstone's owner finally returned to take its cargo back from its burial place?

Jake's eye was still more or less glued to the top of the tombstone. He couldn't move it anymore. He didn't even bother to struggle. He was trapped, and that was that.

Then Jake wiggled his finger.

Wiggle really isn't the word. *Wiggle* suggests a back-and-forth movement. All Jake could do was push his finger a fraction of a centimeter forward. Enough to feel the pad of his fingertip against whatever had been trapping him there.

It was the most he had moved, save for the eye, in days.

A shaft of moonlight stabbed through the dark, shining on his face like a searchlight. Another followed. And another.

Jake knew what was happening. Cracks were reappearing in the surface of the tombstone, as if being cut by an invisible bread slicer. The pieces of the stone jigsaw were being flipped aside by the alien force that had trapped him there.

More light beamed onto his face. He hadn't been using his one good eye, and it wasn't adjusting to even the dim light from the moon and stars. The result was like staring into the sun.

It didn't matter. The core was back in the tombstone!

Not only did it spell his freedom, but it also meant that Darryl and Jonathan had won! Jake blinked his eye shut and found that he could even curl his lips into a smile.

The solid around him started to melt. Jake's body pushed forward through the substance. His muscles, which hadn't done much for a while, started to ache.

Jake tried to stretch, but bolts of pain surged through him. The interior of the tombstone was a liquid now. Jake's head and limbs clunked against the sides of the walls. Every movement was agony, but he had to get out.

A moment later, the liquid began to drain from around

him. Jake felt the top of his head exposed to the freezing night air. A cloud of thick steam poured out of the tomb-stone. The liquid lowered past his ears, his chin, his neck, and Jake's head flopped forward.

The fluid poured out of the prison, and Jake collapsed to the earth with a heavy thud. He could not move. All he could do was feel the vapour pouring off him, feel every nerve in his body as if stung by bees, and wait for life to reclaim him.

Liquid seeped out of his ears. Sounds were thick and heavy, but soon he recognized them as voices. More of the liquid leaked out of his ears, and he could hear a word.

"Jake!"

Jake still couldn't move. His skin and clothes were paint-ed in a jelly-like substance that was already running off his body. He could feel the thick liquid ooze away from him, maybe to rejoin with the rest of the tombstone.

Still, he did not move, even when he felt a hand on his shoulder. A warm, human hand. Gently, it nudged him. There was a voice to go with it, too. "Jake, are you okay? Can you hear me?"

It was Jonathan.

Jake opened his mouth to speak, and heaved out globs of the dark, oozy liquid. His good eye still closed, Jake gasped for breath, but none came. He panted for air, but his wheez-ing hinted at liquid in his air passages. Jake doubled over, and a thick stream of dark snot leaked out of his nostrils and joined the puddle on the ground before him. He coughed again, this time managing to grab a little air, and held it in his lungs. It felt glorious.

He continued this for a few minutes, until all of the liq-uefied stone was out of his system and pooling on the ground before him. Once there, it trailed in a stream back to the tombstone prison, which still loomed menacingly behind him.

Jake found himself staring at the eye, still mounted to the top of the tombstone. He pulled it free of the gum and regarded it quizzically. It didn't seem quite so menacing anymore. He was seeing through both eyes now and was staring at an image of himself, as if looking in a mirror. He looked terrible. His skin had taken on a sickly pallor, although this only came through in patches. He was also still covered in the quickly drying sediment from the tombstone.

Jake's double vision started to get blurry. The image from the once-floating eye was fading. Now that he was no longer in the tombstone or touching any of the dark stone, he couldn't control the eye. There was nothing connecting the eye to his brain anymore — not the muscles or nerves of his body, nor the stone substance. It was just a lifeless thing now.

Jake cradled it in the palm of his hand. Maybe he would be able to see with it again, maybe not. What mattered was that he was still alive.

"Jake …?"

He turned his attention to Jonathan.

Jake blinked his best friend into proper focus. Jonathan didn't look good. His face was battered, with a dark bruise on one cheek and deep scratches gouged into his face.

"What happened?" Jake asked.

"You missed a good fight," Jonathan admitted, his voice shaky and weak. He took a long breath.

Jake's other senses were taking over. He shivered as the cool air chilled his skin. It was a good kind of shiver, because it meant that he could still feel. "Are you okay?"

Jonathan nodded. "I'll live."

Jake now found he could focus on other things, such as the other person standing before him.

It pained Jake to say what he was going to say next. But something had happened to Darryl Richter these past few days. He had been helpful. He had been, Jake gulped at the thought, a *friend*.

"Thanks, Darryl," Jake said. "I couldn't have done this without you."

Darryl nodded. "I'm sorry."

"I know."

"I mean, really, *really* sorry. For all the wedgies, and … you know … everything."

"Thanks for saving my life," Jake returned.

Darryl shrugged. "Anytime," he replied, and turned to Jonathan. They exchanged a knowing stare. It had obviously been a traumatic ordeal for them all.

Together, the three made their way out of the old cemetery, a place Jake vowed never to return to again. They climbed up the hill. Although it would have been nice to take a little extra time because they were so tired, there was still one last thing to deal with.

Jake's parents.

They were standing there, on the other side of the front gate, with arms folded across their chests.

"Just what do you think you're up to?" Jake's mom said angrily.

"Get over here now," Jake's father ordered.

The three boys hopped the fence and shuffled over to Jake's parents.

It took both parents a moment or two to realize that Jonathan and Darryl were looking pretty bruised and battered.

"What kind of mischief have you been up to?" Jake's mom asked.

Darryl shrugged his shoulders. "We, uh, slipped going down the hill."

Jake hadn't realized that his parents had driven Jonathan and Darryl here.

Jake held his hands out defensively. He'd been so preoccupied with stopping Other Jake and its alien kind that he hadn't come up with a story to explain it all. Jake's parents probably didn't realize that Other Jake had been masquerading as their son, but how to explain the gloop on the garage floor that trapped Jonathan and Darryl there, or stealing the car, or even coming here to the cemetery?

It was going to have to be really convincing.

"I can explain everything," Jake lied.

He took a step forward, prepared to come up with the greatest excuse he could imagine, and —

"Jake!"

Jake's mom was looking at her son like she'd seen a ghost.

"What … *happened* to you?" his father added.

Jake looked to Darryl and Jonathan. He thought about everything that had happened with Other Jake. But there was no chance Jake's parents would have been able to find anything out about him. "Er, nothing," he said. "We were just playing a big old game," he added. "You know, about the car and everything. I'm really sorry. It'll never happen again —"

"Who cares about the car?!"

"You don't?" Jake said, the corner of his lips curving into a smile of relief. "I thought you'd be really upset."

"Upset? *Upset?!*" Jake's dad roared in disbelief. He was

waving his arms around frantically, like trying to direct air traffic. "Your eye is missing!"

Jake widened his one good eye. "Oh," Jake started. He reached into his pocket to produce the other one, which he'd stored there to keep it from getting crushed. Who knew what good it was now?

Jake's parents took one look at it and screamed.

"Right," Jake remembered. "*That* eye."

Jake dangled his legs over the edge of the hospital bed. A dull blue curtain had been drawn to separate the bed from the others in the emergency ward. Harsh fluorescent lights shone down on everyone there — Jake, his parents, along with a few nurses who were just too amazed to leave them in peace. The place was quite crowded.

It got even more crowded when the curtain parted and the doctor stepped in.

Jake immediately recognized him. It was the same man who'd treated his scratched eye that had started all of this.

The doctor was busy reading the chart in his hands. "… *patient suffering from missing eye? Is this some kind of a joke?*" The doctor looked up from his paperwork to see Jake and his parents waiting expectantly.

The doctor stared at Jake quizzically. He looked from the chart, and back to Jake.

"It's totally gone," the doctor said.

"Yes," Jake returned.

"We know," Jake's mother added, quite emphatically.

"And it doesn't … hurt?" the doctor said. He didn't look entirely well. He almost looked like he needed a doctor, too.

Jake shook his head. He reached behind himself and

177

produced the missing eye. It was now on an ice pack, staring lifelessly toward the floor. He passed the lone eye over to the doctor.

The doctor looked at the little white orb in his open palm. There was no muscle or tissue connected to it, as there should have been. He looked from the eye, back to Jake's head, focused on the strange cavity in Jake's eye socket, and then back down at the eye in his hand. He shook his head. "This is quite impossible," he said at last, and then added, "medically speaking, of course."

"Can you do anything for my son?" Jake's mother asked, her face creased with worry.

The doctor took a long, deep breath, and then smiled. He reached out to pat Jake's arm gently. "Don't worry," he started, somewhat shakily, "I'm sure you'll be right as rain in no time."

Jake nodded. "Sure thing, but what about you?"

CHAPTER 17

Jake's parents wouldn't be Jake's parents if they didn't force him to go to school the next day, even if he had to wear that stupid eye patch again.

It was a normal day, with one major exception. In Mr. Glick's place was a new supply teacher, Mrs. Hinchcliffe. She was an old lady shaped like a warped pear. She waddled around the class, completely unaware of all the note passing, paper airplanes, and funny faces all of Jake's peers were making behind her back.

One thing she did do was get a caretaker to knock the lock off Mr. Glick's desk drawer. The thing was loaded to the top with all sorts of toys — neon wristbands, spinning blade-like tops. Digging through the small mountain of toys was like going back in time. The further she dug, the older the toys got. Mr. Glick must have been hoarding that stuff for years!

Mrs. Hinchcliffe shook her head, pulling out a toy doll. "These were around when I was a kid," she mused. "Who wants it?"

A classroom's worth of hands shot up.

As it turned out, Mrs. Hinchcliffe was pretty cool. She spent a good hour looking at some of the older toys, passing them around, and talking about the way things were when she was younger.

Jake half-listened, half-dozed. He was tired, and glad that things were going back to normal again, even if he was going to have to make do with only one eye.

Someone passed him a wooden toy car. Jake gave it a cursory glance. He was about to pass it on when his one eye caught sight of something carved into the bottom of the toy.

S.C.

Jake smiled at the initials. He slipped the car into his desk, and knew exactly where to take it after school.

It didn't take any convincing to get Jonathan and Darryl to join Jake in visiting Shawn Crumb after school. Darryl was particularly excited to meet this older dude who'd faced the aliens so many years ago. In fact, Jake almost had to run to keep up with Jonathan and Darryl. The two of them didn't seem to be breaking a sweat, but boy, could they walk fast. "Wait up!" Jake yelped, puppy-like. Darryl and Jonathan turned to see their friend in tow, exchanged glances, and reduced their pace.

"What's up, Jake?" Jonathan asked.

Jake doubled over and caught his breath. "Where are you guys going?"

"Going to see Crumb," Jonathan said, coolly.

"But you're going the long way. It's way faster if we go up Shuter Street."

Darryl nodded. "Jonathan was going to show me the ..." His voice trailed off. He scanned the block, and his eyes lit up. "… The bike shop," Darryl continued, pointing to the store just off the main street ahead. "My bike got banged up pretty good the other day. I need to get a new one."

So this was how it was going down. Now that Darryl and Jonathan had stopped the shape-shifting aliens, they'd become the best of friends. And what was to become of Jake? Jake knew this sort of behaviour in girls. One minute, they were best friends, the next, worst enemies. How many times had Mr. Glick or any of Jake's other teachers had to deal with all the girl teasing, bullying, and best friend meltdowns? Boys never had those kinds of problems.

Or did they? Maybe this was just a part of growing up. Jake was going to have to share his best friend with his best enemy. Was Darryl really an *enemy*? He wasn't teasing Jake now. He'd left his usual posse of Malcolm and Horace behind. It was as if in the last couple of days, Darryl and Jonathan had started up their own dynamic duo, and nobody else was invited. Not even Jake.

"You don't need to go to the bike shop. My dad's pretty good at fixing things," Jake suggested. "We've got a bunch of gear in the garage."

Jonathan narrowed his eyes. "I think we'll leave the garage out of this for now," he said. "We want to steer clear of it, after everything that happened."

"Oh," Jake said, and nodded thoughtfully. "Right." He hadn't considered how spooky this whole ordeal might have been for Jonathan, or even Darryl. It wasn't as if *they'd* been trapped in an alien prison with only a floating eye to glimpse the outside world.

The boys proceeded down the street toward the bike shop. Neither Jonathan nor Darryl spoke a word, so Jake decided to break the silence. "Hey, Jonathan, I still never got an answer, you know, about last night, back at the cemetery."

Jonathan stopped and fixed Jake with a glance that was hard to read. "An answer to what?"

Jake shifted his weight from foot to foot. "What exactly, uh, you know, *happened*?"

Darryl and Jonathan looked at Jake. Neither answered.

Jake licked his lips. They had gone dry, along with his tongue. "You stopped Mr. Glick and the other me, remember? You used the core on them. But *how* did you use it?"

Jonathan shrugged. "What do you mean? I just … used it."

Jake shook his head. "That's not what I'm asking. I also held that core. I never thought it could be used to stop anything. I thought it was just some sort of key for the prison. So what gives? Was there some button you could press on it that shot out a laser beam or something —"

Jonathan nodded quickly. "Yes, that's it. A laser beam. Just like you said."

"Okay, great. But how did it work?"

Jonathan's attention seemed to fixate someplace else. He was staring past Jake, to the grocery store they'd just walked by.

"Jonathan, are you even listening to me?!"

One of the cashiers was standing outside, her attention focused on the three boys. Seeing them there, she broke out into an unusual, knowing smile, and gave them a wave.

Jake looked over his shoulder. There was no one else for her to wave to. He wrinkled his brow. "Who is that?"

Neither Jonathan nor Darryl answered him. They were too busy waving back to the cashier.

"Uh, guys?"

Eventually, Darryl and Jonathan turned to Jake, exactly in unison.

Panic surged through Jake. Something was wrong with Jonathan and Darryl, the way they'd been hanging out together all day long.

"Hey guys," Jake continued, "about what happened in the cemetery …"

"We defeated the aliens," Darryl said.

"They are no longer a threat," Jonathan added.

Heart hammering in his chest, Jake took a step back. He shook his head in disbelief.

All Jonathan and Darryl did was smile. They were wide smiles, wider than any human smile ought to be. Smiles that took up nearly their whole faces.

Darryl clasped Jake by the wrist and squeezed.

Jonathan smiled even wider, so that Jake could see the row of sharp little teeth behind the human ones.

"Don't worry, Jake," he said softly. "Everything will be right as rain in no time."

THINGS YOU SHOULD KNOW ABOUT
JEFF SZPIRGLAS

Jeff Szpirglas knows about all of the things that terrify you.

Seriously. Do you think your innermost fears and secrets are safe? Sorry, they're not. Jeff knows them. Don't ask how. He just does.

Jeff has written numerous non-fiction books, including the award-nominated *Fear This Book*, *Gross Universe*, and *You Just Can't Help It!* Jeff has also written for CBC radio, television, and was the kids' page editor at *Chirp*, *chickaDEE*, and *OWL* magazines.

Jeff hails from Hamilton, Ontario, but now makes his home in Toronto. He has one wife, two cats, and several plants that are still not dead. By day, he teaches at an elementary school. By night, he will haunt you.

This is his first novel.

RECEIVED

JUN 1 7 2013

BY:

CPSIA information can be obtained at www.ICGtesting.com
Printed in the USA
LVOW131359060613

PP7602500001B/2/P

9 780986 791475